FROM THE NANCY DREW FILES

THE CASE: Nancy goes behind the cameras to focus on a ten-million-dollar Hollywood blackmailing scheme.

CONTACT: Director James Jackson, *an old friend of Carson Drew, casts Nancy in the role of criminal investigator.*

SUSPECTS: Susie Yaeger—*The movie's producer fears the film will bomb . . . unless she can create some sensational publicity.*

David Raymond—*The film's co-star complains that he's underpaid, but he may have found a way to balance the books.*

Danielle Wilner—*She's in charge of special effects . . . and what could be more special than a ten-million-dollar payoff?*

COMPLICATIONS: *The blackmail plot thickens when the title of the movie—Dangerous Loves— seems to mirror Nancy's own L.A. story.*

Books in the Nancy Drew Files™ Series

Available from ARCHWAY Paperbacks

THE
NANCY DREW FILES™

120

DANGEROUS LOVES

CAROLYN KEENE

AN ARCHWAY PAPERBACK
Published by POCKET BOOKS
New York London Toronto Sydney Tokyo Singapore

AN ARCHWAY PAPERBACK *Original*

 An Archway Paperback published by
POCKET BOOKS, a division of Simon & Schuster Inc.
1230 Avenue of the Americas, New York, NY 10020

Copyright © 1997 by Simon & Schuster Inc.
Produced by Mega-Books, Inc.

ISBN: 0-671-56878-7

First Archway Paperback printing April 1997

10 9 8 7 6 5 4 3 2 1

NANCY DREW, AN ARCHWAY PAPERBACK and colophon are registered trademarks of Simon & Schuster Inc.

THE NANCY DREW FILES is a trademark of Simon & Schuster Inc.

Cover art by Bill Schmidt

Printed in the U.S.A.

IL 6+

Chapter

One

SMOKED SALMON? Caviar?" The flight attendant pushed the food cart alongside Nancy Drew's seat.

Nancy's blue eyes shot a challenge toward her best friend, George Fayne. She flipped back her reddish blond hair and asked, "Well? Should we go for it?"

"Why not?" George responded. She smoothed out her khaki pants and patted her stomach. "Isn't that what flying first class is all about?"

Nancy smiled at the flight attendant. "One of everything, please."

Within moments Nancy and George were staring at a beautiful array of hors d'oeuvres arranged on china plates.

"This is great," George said between bites. She motioned toward the clouds floating by like

1

mountains of cotton outside the window. "Maybe we can just keep flying back and forth between River Heights and Hollywood forever. The food beats burgers and fries any day, and you can't top this view."

Nancy laughed. "I'm not exactly sure how we'd finance that life-style," she said, taking a bite of smoked salmon. "Dad's generous, not crazy." Carson Drew had been Nancy's biggest fan and source of support ever since her mother had died, fifteen years earlier.

Nancy's joking expression shifted to one of concern. "And actually we're flying first class because James Jackson insisted on it. He needs our help. He's in serious trouble."

"You never explained exactly what kind of trouble," George said.

Nancy sighed and began. "Well, you already know Jackson is an old friend of my father."

George nodded. "And he's also the film director who made *Me and My Rolls* and *A Taste to Die For.* I've seen all his films."

"George . . . " Nancy lowered her voice and leaned toward her friend. "Mr. Jackson is being blackmailed." George's eyes opened wide, but she said nothing.

"He was desperate when he called my father," Nancy continued. "He didn't know what to do. He's gotten a number of threatening messages from someone demanding ten million dollars or—"

"Or what?" George asked.

2

"Or the newspapers are going to get word of a horrible scandal Mr. Jackson was involved in many years ago. It's old news, but he thinks it could ruin his career if it makes its way into the headlines now."

"And he wanted you to investigate?"

Nancy laughed and shook her head. "That's not exactly why he called. I think he just wanted to vent a little to my dad. But I was sitting right there, so I couldn't help overhearing part of the conversation."

"And you offered to help."

"It took a little work, but I finally convinced them to let me give the case a try. And, of course, I needed a travel companion," Nancy said, grinning at her friend.

"Hollywood, here we come!" George said. She tossed her short dark curls, raised her head, and struck a movie-star pose.

One in-flight movie and a three-star meal later, the pilot's voice came over the loudspeaker system. "Folks, we're currently circling Los Angeles. Ground conditions are a breezy seventy-two degrees."

As the plane touched down, Nancy's thoughts were already on the case. If she couldn't find the blackmailer, James Jackson would have to pay ten million dollars—or risk the biggest humiliation of his career.

Nancy and George deplaned and stepped into the passageway that connected the aircraft to the terminal. They walked down a long corridor, past the point where people who were on departing flights were having their luggage X-rayed. There, a small group of people, some with signs, waited for passengers on arriving flights.

Nancy scanned the crowd, and she quickly caught sight of a short, dark-haired man holding a sign with her name on it. She smiled and waved at him.

"I'm Liam O'Connell, Mr. Jackson's personal assistant." He showed Nancy his license as identification and then reached for the girls' carry-on bags. "Did you check any luggage?" he asked.

"No," Nancy said. "We just have the carry-ons."

"Then we can go straight to the car," Liam said, heading toward the exit.

"Mr. Jackson wanted to meet you personally," Liam explained as the girls followed him, "but the crowds at the airport . . . well, sometimes it's tricky for him. He's asked me to drive you back to the house."

"Is our hotel near his house?" Nancy asked.

"Hotel? Oh, no. You'll be staying at the Jacksons' home."

Nancy and George grinned at each other. Everyone had read about James Jackson's incredible mansion. Among its luxurious features were a movie theater and a ten-pin bowling alley.

Minutes later Nancy and George were sitting in the back of Mr. Jackson's limousine. As Liam drove through downtown Los Angeles, he pointed out spots of interest among the low, square office buildings. As the car began to climb into the hills, the buildings gave way to private homes and then to larger and larger mansions.

"That used to be Ellen Hyde's house—you know, the silent film star." Liam pointed toward an elegant estate.

"I hope we'll get to catch some of the sights," George said. "I'd at least like to put my hand in some of those famous handprints on the Walk of Fame."

"Yeah. Judy Garland, Marilyn Monroe, all those fabulous stars. We'll see," Nancy said, not sounding too hopeful.

"How about surfing? Venice Beach? And there's always—"

"Hold on, George. One thing at a time," Nancy teased. "I have a feeling we'll be pretty busy, anyway."

It wasn't long before the limousine drove through a pair of wrought-iron gates and up a long, curving driveway. In front of the huge house with its tall white pillars and dozens of windows stood a short, balding man wearing jeans, a black button-down shirt, and a tweed jacket with elbow patches. Liam pulled to a stop.

"That's James Jackson," George whispered.

"Thanks, George, I'd never have guessed," Nancy said, rolling her eyes.

Next to Mr. Jackson stood a tall, willowy blond wearing a stylish suit and a long string of pearls. Nancy recognized James Jackson's wife, a

5

famous actress—whom Nancy knew by her stage name, Raye Brodburne—and a teenage girl with high cheekbones, wearing a short black dress that showed off her long, slender legs.

Nancy knew the girl was the Jacksons' daughter, Lori, a popular television actress. Though she was only eighteen, Lori was already well on her way to stardom, making the jump to the big screen as the lead in her father's current project, *Dangerous Loves.*

Liam got out of the limo, opened the back door for Nancy and George, then whisked their luggage inside. George hung back, seeming a bit nervous, but Nancy smiled confidently and stepped toward the famous family.

"Hello, I'm Nancy Drew," she said.

"Oh, Nancy, we would have recognized you in a second from the pictures your father has sent us over the years," James Jackson said.

"I recognize you from your pictures, too, Mr. Jackson," Nancy said, meaning, of course, the ones she had seen in newspapers and magazines. She extended her hand toward him.

Instead of taking it, James Jackson pulled her into a big bear hug. "No need to be formal," he said. "Please call me James."

Nancy smiled. "Okay . . . James." She introduced George, and in turn, James Jackson introduced his wife and daughter.

"We're so grateful you could come," his wife said warmly. "Your father says you're the best detective he knows, and that's just what we need right now."

"We sure do," Lori agreed. She flashed Nancy a Hollywood smile.

"They're right," the director said. "We're all glad you could come." His smile disappeared briefly, and he sighed, with what Nancy could only interpret as anxiety and weariness. In the next moment, however, his face reflected gracious charm once again.

This must be killing him, Nancy thought. Trying to keep it all together in front of his family—in front of George and me—when his entire career is on the line.

James motioned toward the house. "Let me show you around," he said. Nancy stood for a moment looking at the outside of the house, with its long, elegant portico and tall, graceful columns. Bright, showy flowers blossomed in a garden that ran the length of the massive front lawn. At one side was a huge open garage that held a red Maserati, among half a dozen expensive vehicles.

James took George on one arm and Nancy on the other and led them inside the house.

The entryway was vast and elegant, the area anchored in the middle by a granite pedestal on which sat a huge bouquet of fresh flowers in an ebony vase. A grand staircase led to an upper floor of the home.

"Would you like to see the place?" Lori asked.

"Would we ever!" George exclaimed, and grinned at Nancy.

Lori, followed by her mother and father, led the girls along wide polished oak-floored corridors. In addition to a huge living room with a fireplace and an elegant dining room, Lori showed the girls an English-style library straight out of a Jane Austen novel, and an entertainment room with a television screen that covered an entire wall, as well as two offices and a wicker-filled sunporch. Nancy and George followed, somewhat in a daze.

"Don't worry." Lori's mother smiled as she noticed the girls' startled looks. "You'll find your way around the house before you know it."

"It's like going to a new high school," Lori commented. "At first you're always getting lost, and you can't even find your locker, but soon you know it like the back of your hand."

"Could we finish the tour a bit later?" James Jackson interrupted. "Right now, I'd like a private moment with Nancy." He turned to Lori. "Princess, could you show George to the guest wing?"

"Sure, Daddy."

"See you in a bit, Nancy," George said over her shoulder as she and Lori headed off down yet another corridor.

James motioned Nancy into his study. He sank into one of two black leather couches, and Nancy sat in another. Through the tall French doors of the study, she could see yet another beautiful flower garden.

James let out a heavy sigh. "I wish I had better news." Gone was his cheerful expression.

"Mr. Jackson—James," Nancy said, "you know I'll do my best to help you."

James managed a tired smile. "I hope you can," he said. "You know that someone has been sending me threatening messages demanding a ridiculously huge sum of money. For a while I wrote it off as an annoying prank."

"But?" Nancy prompted.

"But recently the notes have made it clear that the blackmailer isn't kidding around. He or she has information about me—personal information—that could ruin me."

Nancy was silent for a moment. Then she said, "If I'm going to help you, I'll need to know the details—the personal details."

James held Nancy in his gaze for a moment. "I know I can trust you."

He leaned back, closed his eyes, and began his story. "It happened thirty years ago. I'd already made a few hit movies, but I wasn't married yet. I was summering at a beach resort on Rapid Island. There were starlets, parties that went on for days—the works. One night, I was driving around with a young actress in her car—I was at the wheel—and we decided to drive over the bridge between the resort and the mainland. It was such a small thing, foolish, really. I swerved to avoid some animal in the road. But the surface was oily, slick with rain, and I lost control of the car." Nancy watched him closely as he spoke. His face looked old and sad.

"We didn't make it," James said. "Halfway over the bridge, I plowed through the guardrail, and we crashed into the bay."

"How terrible!" Nancy exclaimed, feeling dread in the pit of her stomach. "What happened to the actress?"

James looked into Nancy's eyes and shook his head. "Bianca didn't know how to swim. I tried to find her, but it was dark, and I couldn't locate her in the water. Bianca drowned." He took a deep breath, and Nancy saw tears in his eyes.

What a tragedy. How could it be that she had never heard anything about it before? It was the kind of thing that tabloid magazines loved to bring up—over and over and over again, no matter how many years had passed.

"There's no question it was my fault," James said, agonized. "And then I made things worse. I covered it up. I told the police Bianca was driving, and since it was her car, they believed me. As a result, no charges were ever brought against me. And more important, the story never went beyond the local newspapers. That would have ruined me. And, Nancy, it still could."

"But how? It was an accident. And you tried to help Bianca," Nancy noted.

James shook his head. "That wouldn't matter. If anyone ever found out I was driving, I'd be ruined. The tabloids would make me out to be a monster. And you know, they wouldn't be totally wrong. After all, it *was* my fault we crashed.

"Anyway," James continued, "that was all in the past. Or I thought it was. Then, a few weeks ago, the messages started. Last week, the black-mailer mentioned Rapid Island and told me to pay up. Ten million dollars!"

Nancy nodded. She already knew about the money. "And who knew about the incident at the time?"

James pressed his lips together. "Rapid Island is a small place. I'd say no one knew anything at all. Bianca's family, the people at the hospital, and the coroner all believed it was a tragic accident—that she had been behind the wheel of her car and had crashed through the guardrail. They didn't know about my part in it."

"And have you confided in anyone in all the years since the accident?"

James thought for a moment. "Well, my wife, of course. And since the threats started, my daughter." He looked ashamed. "But that's it. I have never mentioned it to a soul outside my family."

Nancy sighed. She didn't say so to James, but it didn't really matter. There was surely a record of the incident at the Rapid Island Police Department, small as it was. Any decent snoop could get at that information, as well as dig up a local newspaper article. If James had ever even hinted that something had happened that long-ago summer, it could have been enough to tip off his blackmailer.

James hit the arm of the leather couch with a frustrated slap. "Nancy, I'd pay the ten million—if I had it. But I don't. You may not believe this, but I'm just about broke."

"Broke?" Nancy thought about the huge house, the Maserati, the other expensive vehicles, the servants, the first-class plane tickets.

"Oh, sure, I've made enough to set up this Hollywood life-style." He gestured around the room and shook his head bitterly. "But cash? I don't have much of that left. I've sunk every penny into this house and my film. I couldn't scare up ten million if my life depended on it. And it does."

"But you're James Jackson," Nancy broke in. "The films you've directed have been huge hits all over the world."

James gave Nancy a slight smile. "So you've seen my movies," he said.

"Yes," Nancy answered. "They're terrific."

"But *where* have you seen them?"

Nancy thought for a moment, confused. Then, she understood what he was getting at. "Well, mostly on the late-night shows on TV," she admitted.

"Exactly," James said. "I haven't had a box-office hit in a decade. I'm famous, I've made several films in recent years, but I haven't made a successful film in a long time."

"Don't you get residuals or percentages or something?" Nancy asked.

"Certainly not to the tune of ten million dollars. I just don't have the money."

Nancy looked at the man who was one of her father's oldest friends. He seemed lost in thought.

"Let's talk about suspects," Nancy said. "Do you have any enemies? Anyone you think might have learned about the Rapid Island incident?"

James shook his head. "I know I'm not perfect," he joked, "but for a film director, I'm a pretty nice guy. No big enemies. No Hollywood infighting. I do have a producer right now whom I'd like to strangle, and I'm pretty sure she'd like to strangle me."

Before Nancy had a chance to ask another question, a bloodcurdling scream ripped through the mansion, instantly bringing Nancy and James to their feet.

Chapter

Two

THAT'S RAYE!" James shouted. In an instant, he was racing down the hallway.

Nancy followed him through the corridors of the house and up a flight of stairs to a huge bedroom. Mrs. Jackson was standing in the middle of the room, quivering and as white as a sheet.

"S-someone sent me fl-flowers," she stuttered.

She pointed at a long box that lay open on the thick white carpet. Two dozen long-stemmed red roses were scattered about as if the box had been dropped. Among the roses, something moved. James stepped closer to look. Then he jumped back as a huge snake emerged from beneath the flowers.

"Don't panic," he said. He grabbed a heavy

book from the bedstand and prepared to pound the snake with it.

Nancy grabbed his uplifted arm. "Hold on," she said. "I don't think you need to do that. It's a boa constrictor, and they're only dangerous when angry or frightened. And they're *not* poisonous."

"You're sure?" James asked.

Nancy nodded and motioned at the snake, which now lay very still. "Really, it's a very gentle creature. If we don't hurt it, we'll be fine."

James slowly lowered the book and set it on the bed. The snake looked grotesquely out of place in the gracious surroundings. The walls were covered with a soft floral-pattern fabric, and a gentle breeze coming in off the balcony prompted a dancing movement of the matching draperies.

Mrs. Jackson slipped over to Nancy, carefully avoiding the boa. "What a thing to happen your first evening at our house," she said. "I was hoping to be able to be a civilized hostess and show you the sights of L.A. before you delve into this horrible mess of ours. But it looks as though James's blackmailer is taking his task more seriously with each passing day."

"I'd better check my E-mail," James said, abruptly turning to leave the room. "Let's shut the snake up in this room till we figure out what to do with it." Nancy and Raye followed. Then James closed the door behind them.

As James headed back toward his study, Nancy looked at Raye. "E-mail?" Nancy whispered. "At a time like this? James seems pretty self-possessed about this—already going back to business?"

"No, you see, that's how the blackmailer has been contacting him," Raye explained, following her husband. "I'm sure James will have a message waiting for him, claiming responsibility for this little gift I just got."

Raye was obviously still a bit shaken, and Nancy took her arm as they walked.

In his office, James booted up his computer. He hit a few buttons, typed in his password, and pulled up his E-mail box. Sure enough, it held a message.

"Come here, Nancy. Take a look," he insisted, his face set in a grimace.

Nancy read over his shoulder:

By now my little pet has slithered into your life. He's not poisonous—but he's got friends who are. Ten million bucks will ensure that none of them will pay you a visit.

Nancy felt a quick chill run down her spine.

"I knew it," James said, his voice trembling. He held his head in his hands and massaged his temples. "Shooting *Dangerous Loves* would be stressful enough without all this," he went on. "But I worry all the time about my career and about my family." He stood and approached his

16

wife, then wrapped his arms around her. "I've put you and Lori in danger," he said. "For that, I just can't forgive myself."

Raye shut her eyes and held her husband close, as if trying to absorb all his troubles and make everything better. He stroked her hair absently.

Nancy stepped out of the study to give the couple a moment to themselves just as George came pounding down the hall.

"Nancy, what happened? I was unpacking in my room, and I thought I heard screams," George said.

Nancy quickly caught George up on the details of the director's situation and told her about the delivery of the boa constrictor.

"Things are heating up fast on this one," George commented, frowning.

"Mmmm," Nancy agreed. "That was no garden variety snake."

"I guess this rules out surfing for the moment," George said good-naturedly.

"By the way, where's Lori?" Nancy asked. "I'm surprised she didn't hear her mother screaming."

"Probably because she's taking a shower," George replied. "She said she needed to get ready because she's shooting a scene later."

Just then the Jacksons joined the girls in the hallway.

"Well, I'm not sure what to do about the boa," Nancy said. "Maybe we should start calling pet stores to see if there's one that would take it."

James Jackson, who was looking somewhat better now, waved his hand toward the bedroom. "Oh, actually, now that I've had a moment to collect my thoughts, I bet Danielle can help us out."

"Who's Danielle?" Nancy asked.

"Danielle Wilner, my special effects coordinator for *Dangerous Loves,*" James explained. "Among other strange attributes, she's a big snake person. I'm sure she'll take this fellow off our hands."

Nancy shot George a look that said, We're onto something. Out loud she asked, "Can I meet Danielle?"

James nodded. "Sure, you and George can come along with us later this afternoon. Lori and I have to head back to the set and shoot a scene."

"Yes, George just told me that Lori's in a scene later," Nancy said. She was pleased to get started on a lead. If Danielle Wilner was into snakes, Nancy wanted to check her out. And she had to admit, too, she was excited to be able to see the filming of *Dangerous Loves* on her very first night in L.A. "George and I will need cover stories for why we're on the set," she said.

"Of course," James agreed.

"Darling," his wife said, "don't you think Nancy and George could work as extras in the crowd scenes? That might be a good cover." The director's wife winked at Nancy and George.

He clapped his hands. "Wonderful, wonderful. Why didn't I think of that immediately."

18

George gave Nancy a high five. "All right!" she said.

Nancy laughed. Too bad Bess isn't here, she thought. This is right up her alley. Nancy's other best friend, Bess Marvin, was off visiting relatives. She loved acting and would have enjoyed this small shot at stardom. No doubt she'd have developed a crush on one or two handsome actors, as well.

The Jacksons decided to calm down with tea on the back terrace. George and Nancy declined the offer, so George showed Nancy to the guest wing. They marveled at the plush bedrooms they'd be staying in. Nancy started unpacking the suitcases Liam had deposited there earlier, and George threw herself down on the gorgeous sleigh bed.

"This is incredible, isn't it?" George said, looking around at the lavish draperies, the oriental rugs, the fresh flowers. Nancy's room was considerably smaller than the Jacksons' but just as tastefully decorated. "And this is just a guest room! I could sure get used to it in a hurry," she said, lounging on the bed.

Nancy laughed from inside the room's enormous walk-in closet. The few clothes she'd hung up looked pretty lonely in there, she thought. "It's a far cry from River Heights, that's for sure," she agreed, walking back out into the main room. "But if things don't improve for James, the Jacksons might not be living this way much longer."

"Yeah. It's really a shame that something truly accidental that happened so long ago could threaten James's future and that of his family," said George. "You've got to feel sorry for the man."

An hour later Nancy, George, Lori and James were heading for the set of *Dangerous Loves*. Nancy had told Lori about the snake. Liam, whose job as personal assistant seemed to cover a number of duties, had managed to pack the boa back in the flower box, provide it with some airholes, and load it into the trunk before they left. On the way to the set, James explained the plot of the film to the girls as Lori drove his car, a dark green sedan.

"It's 1945. An army nurse, played by Lori, awaits the return of her soldier sweetheart from World War II. The soldier is played by David Raymond."

Nancy, who was sitting in front, looked over at Lori as she recalled a few magazine articles she had read lately about Lori and David. They had been a big item for about six months until their recent breakup, and the ups and downs of their relationship had been the subject of tabloid headlines for weeks. Lori's face showed nothing, but her knuckles were clenched white around the steering wheel.

James continued. "When the soldier arrives, everything is wonderful. He proposes, and they plan to get married. But as time goes on, Lori's character begins to have reservations about the man's character. He's behaving erratically, one minute the adoring fiancé, the next angry, almost violent. When he won't explain his strange absences to her, she breaks off the romance. He begins to stalk her."

Nancy watched Lori carefully as she executed a turn off the freeway.

"Sometimes, movies are a little too much like real life," Lori said.

Chapter

Three

DID LORI MEAN David Raymond was stalking her? Nancy wondered. Was he really a dangerous man? She knew now wasn't the time to ask Lori any more about her ex-boyfriend, but Nancy would be sure to keep Lori's strange comment in mind when she met the male lead.

As Lori steered the car through the studio gate, she waved at the guard and drove toward a group of trailers at the back of the set. There were a lot of people milling around. The place gave no sign of the trouble that was plaguing the film's director.

"How does the movie end?" George asked eagerly.

"Maybe I should make you buy a ticket and see it in the movie theater to find out," James said with a laugh. "Here we are at the set, anyway. I'll finish the plot later." They parked in a spot reserved for Mr. Jackson. As Nancy and George got out of the car, they soaked up their first view of the set.

Nancy felt as if they'd stepped straight into another place and time. They were standing on the edge of a reproduction of a city street, circa 1945. Sleek, old-fashioned cars lined the curb. A movie marquis announced Alfred Hitchcock's *Spellbound,* starring Ingrid Bergman and Gregory Peck. Extras stood about expectantly, the women carefully costumed in narrow skirts and stylish hats, the men in slouchy suits and fedoras. Everything was so convincingly set back in time that it startled Nancy to see a couple of the extras eating out of modern fast-food wrappers. One soldier was sitting on a stoop, wearing headphones and moving to the beat of the music playing on his portable CD player.

James smiled when he saw Nancy's and George's obvious wonder. "Feels like you're right there, doesn't it?" he said, leading them toward a tented dressing area. There, a costume mistress and her assistant were working with the extras.

Moments later Nancy and George were being measured and fitted. The seamstress silently pinned the clothes where they didn't quite fit, then sewed them up with long basting stitches.

When they'd each been fitted with three outfits that were tagged and catalogued with their names, they were accessorized with hats, handbags, and shoes.

"Aren't you loving this?" George asked.

"You bet," Nancy said. "Beats seeing the sights, wouldn't you say?"

Next they visited the makeup artist, who expertly smoothed their faces with pancake makeup and powder, and penciled their eyebrows in a classic 1940s' arch. Bright red lipstick completed the look. Nancy and George exchanged grins as they gave themselves the once-over in a full-length mirror.

"If Ned could see me now, he'd be doing his Humphrey Bogart imitation for sure," Nancy said with a laugh. Nancy's longtime boyfriend, Ned Nickerson, attended Emerson College. Nancy knew he'd appreciate her new look.

"I can just imagine," George said, rolling her eyes. "Did you see how fast that makeup person put these faces on us? Bess could take a few lessons from her—just think how much time we'd save waiting for her to get her makeup on right."

As they stepped out of the tent, James walked over from where he'd been consulting with a production person. He placed a hand on Nancy's shoulder. "Well, ladies, how does it feel to be making your film debut?"

Nancy beamed. "It's great!"

"You both look lovely. We'll have to get lots of photos for you to take home with you as mementos of your visit." He paused. "I truly hope there'll be good reason for you to have fond memories of the City of Angels, but I have to say I mean that rather selfishly. George, I'm going to borrow Nancy for a little while." He turned to Nancy. "It's probably time you met Susie Yaeger, our esteemed producer."

"Good. I'll need to meet everyone you're involved with on the set." Nancy waved to George. "You'll be okay on your own, right?"

"Yeah, I'm fine—except for these stockings." She fidgeted with the seams that ran up the backs of her legs. "After I have a look around, I'll wait for you near the movie theater."

As James and Nancy headed off, lighting people hurried around, readjusting lights on high tripods. A second crew set up a series of cameras positioned around the spot where the scene was to be shot. James explained that the cameras would be used to shoot the scene from various angles. Yet another crew checked the rainmaking machines. Nancy was impressed by the number of people it took to film a single scene.

Lori stood off at one side of the commotion, looking gorgeous even in the baggy 1945 army nurse's uniform she was wearing. A stylist rushed over to her every few minutes to make sure that her makeup and hair remained camera-ready.

As they walked by, Nancy noticed that Lori looked agitated, fidgeting with her hair, and shifting back and forth from one pump to the other. Nancy wondered again about the comment Lori had muttered back in the car. Did

David pose more of a threat than anyone realized?

"Adjust that camera dolly . . . tilt those lights away from the others." James Jackson jolted Nancy's attention back to the present moment. He walked through the set as if it was his living room, calmly attending to a variety of details as casually as he would fix himself a sandwich.

They walked on, and he spoke quietly to Nancy. "Susie and I don't get along too well."

Nancy looked at the director and tried to read his face. "Do you think she might have something to do with your problem?"

James nodded slowly. "Could be. Susie was Bianca's best friend. I'm not sure Susie knows about the—about what happened all those years ago. But . . . well, I suspect."

Nancy stared at James Jackson as he spoke. Bianca and Susie Yaeger were best friends? That's no small detail that he neglected to mention earlier, she thought.

"Why don't you get along? Has she ever said anything to you about Bianca?" Nancy probed.

"Sure, she's mentioned Bianca plenty of times. She knew I dated her occasionally, and she didn't like it. She thought I was too wild. Hard to imagine now," he said, running a hand over his balding head. "Anyway, she even knew we were supposed to see each other the night of the accident. But she's never said anything specific about it, about that night, I mean. She's just always seemed angry at me, as if she suspects that I was behind the wheel that night."

Nancy could see James's face cloud over. "Oh, Nancy. I just wish none of it had ever happened. I wish I'd handled it all differently. To have the death of a friend on my head all these years, the guilt, and now the threats to my family. Sometimes, I can hardly bear to see my own face staring back at me in the mirror."

"James, it was an accident, it wasn't your fault," Nancy said. But she knew that nothing short of putting a stop to the blackmailer once and for all would be of any comfort to James.

They moved away from the set toward another cluster of trailers. Around them, boxes were stacked, each marked as to what piece of set or prop it contained. Clearly, this was organized chaos, but Nancy had to shake her head at the sheer volume of chaos. Someone drove by in a golf cart stacked with long sheets of plywood.

"So, how did you and Susie end up working together on *Dangerous Loves*?" Nancy wondered.

James shrugged wearily. "She didn't *want* me to direct this film. But one of the studio execs insisted on me. And, well, I needed the money too badly to say no."

"Hey, genius," a clear male voice called out.

Nancy turned to see an extraordinary-looking young man hurrying toward them. He had piercing green eyes and thick red hair, handsomely chiseled features, and an appealingly relaxed style. Light freckles peppered his cheeks. Nancy figured him to be in his mid-twenties.

The worried look on James's face melted away, and he broke into a grin. "Trent!" The director reached out to shake the young man's hand. "I want you to meet Nancy Drew. She's an old friend of the family, and she's going to be an extra."

James turned to Nancy. "Nancy, this man is the real genius. This is Trent Marino. He wrote the screenplay for *Dangerous Loves*. He's a terrific guy. This movie is a true collaboration between the two of us." He gave Trent a friendly slap on the back.

A grin spread across Trent's handsome face, and he laughed. "Don't you believe this guy. It's his movie, and don't you forget it," he said good-naturedly.

Looking into Trent's sparkling green eyes, Nancy caught her breath. It wasn't that Trent fit in the "devastatingly handsome" category, but Nancy couldn't help noticing his unusual good looks. She sneaked a second glance at Trent and found that he was looking at her, smiling.

James Jackson went on, unaware of the moment that had passed between Nancy and Trent. "Trent's a great writer," he said. "I've made two of his screenplays into films already—*Me and My Rolls* and *A Taste to Die For*. Trent's seen quite a bit of success, especially for such a young man. The sky's the limit for this kind of talent, eh, Trent?"

Trent shifted his weight from one leg to the other, apparently a little embarrassed. "The first time my agent called to say James was interested, I felt as though I'd won the lottery."

James frowned. "Too bad we didn't win the lottery." He turned to Nancy. "The critics loved those movies, but they did miserably at the box office."

Trent smiled and shook his head. "It doesn't matter, James. That was then, this is now." He clasped the director's shoulder affectionately. "This time, we'll rake it in," he said.

"Listen, have you seen Susie?" James asked.

Trent gave a nod of his head toward one of the trailers. "She's in there."

Nancy saw that Trent had gestured toward the trailer with "James Jackson, Director. Private" painted on the door.

James did not look pleased. "See you, Trent." He abruptly ended the conversation and turned toward his trailer.

"I hope to see you again, Nancy," Trent called out with a wave and a smile as he walked away.

James took the three metal stairs to his trailer in one giant step and pushed open the door without knocking. Nancy followed. Inside, a heavyset brunette with a few streaks of gray in her hair was leaning back in a leather reclining chair, her feet crossed on the top of a messy, paper-strewn desk. She was talking animatedly into a cellular telephone and waving a manicured hand adorned with a couple of expensive-looking rings.

"Can't you read the sign on the door?" James growled at the woman. Susie Yaeger, Nancy assumed.

Susie waved her hand. "Please, Jackson. Can't you wait until I get off the phone?" She returned to her call and talked for a few more moments as if no one were in the room. She finished, folded up the phone with a definitive click, then turned to glare at the director. She offered no apology and gave not a hint of acknowledgment of Nancy's presence.

"Jackson," she said, swinging her feet to the floor, "we're only halfway through the shoot, and you're already over budget. What are you going to do about it?"

James turned his back and paced the length of the trailer.

"Come on, come on, come on," Susie said, smacking the back of one hand against the palm of the other.

"Look, we've been over this before," he said, obviously exasperated. "You already know about the few cuts I feel comfortable making. I'd be happy to talk to you about it later—when we're *alone.*" He nodded toward Nancy.

"Later, later," she snapped. "It's always later with you, James. But then, we never do get around to talking."

"Well, maybe that's because you never *talk*. You yell."

"You'd yell, too, if you were the one who had to keep coming up with more cash."

"Oh, come on, Susie, have a little faith. We'll make everything back at the box office."

Susie tossed back her graying hair impatiently. "Maybe we will. Maybe we won't. It's not as though your track record lately promises any such thing."

James swallowed hard. Nancy could see the tension on his face. She knew how heavily this fact weighed on him.

"Look, I know the last couple of films haven't done that well—"

"They disappeared pronto from the theaters and practically went straight to video and television. And we're not talking about just the last two films here, James."

He sighed in frustration. "I guess we're just not the best pair to work together," he said.

"No, we're not," Susie agreed. "You're bad luck, my friend, and frankly I didn't want to have anything to do with you. But until the movie's over, we're stuck being together."

James nodded. "Okay. So let's figure out how we can compromise on the budget."

Susie shook her head emphatically. "Come to my office and scan the budget spreadsheets, if you like. I'm at my bottom line now, Jackson." She stood up and leaned menacingly toward James, her hands planted on the desk. "And I *am* the producer, which makes me your boss. We haven't forgotten that little fact, have we?"

Nancy noticed that James seemed to be struggling to remain composed. Finally, he said quietly, "Okay. I'll *try* to cut some more scenes. If I can."

But Susie wouldn't leave well enough alone. "You do that," she said snidely. "And please, try to come out with a picture audiences are willing to pay to see. My reputation's riding on this one, too, El Director, and I'm not about to let you drag me down. Believe me, I'll do what I have to to make this film a hit."

Susie picked up her shoulder bag and headed toward the trailer door. Her hand on the knob, she stopped, turned, and leveled a look at James. "Your films the last few years have had the stench of death on them, wouldn't you say, Jimmy? And I think you know exactly what I mean." The door shut behind her with a sharp click.

Nancy reached out and touched James Jackson's shoulder, and he smiled thinly. Hollywood is one rough town, Nancy thought. She could tell that Susie's parting words had hit like a bucket of icy water. Was her comment an arch reference to box-office bombs, or was the producer pointedly reminding James of the death of her friend?

Nancy was about to ask James more about Susie's relationship with Bianca, when a strange shout came from the direction of the set.

"What's that?" Nancy asked. "Have they started shooting already?"

"Not without me, and that's not part of the scene, anyway. Come on, let's go," James said, opening the trailer door.

He and Nancy rushed out of the trailer not far behind Susie, who had headed at a gallop toward the direction of the cry.

They rounded a corner and stopped short at the sight of George, in a tight, fierce fighting stance, poised to strike out at a young man in front of her.

"Keeee-yah!" George shouted, before aiming a kick at the man's head.

Chapter

Four

N O!" JAMES YELLED, finally finding his voice. Nancy realized that the small group watching George and her prey had been stunned into silence.

"George, that's David Raymond—"

But it was too late. George's foot was about to connect with the million-dollar face of the star of *Dangerous Loves*.

The actor dodged George's kick but spun around and fell on the gravel. "Ow!" he wailed, wrapping his hands around his knee.

"Oh, I'm so sorry," George said, covering her face with her hands. She rushed over to the young man and tried to help him up, but he quickly stood and moved away from her.

James stepped in. "George, this is David Raymond. I'm surprised you didn't recognize him from his TV series." There was an edge of anger in his voice.

George looked weak with embarrassment. "I recognize him now," she said.

Nancy did, too. He had thick black hair and full, round lips that Nancy would wager nine out of ten girls would recognize. She had only seen him on television, but she could see he was even more handsome in person.

"What is this chick's problem?" David demanded as he brushed dust and gravel off his pants and glared at George.

"It was a simple misunderstanding, David," Lori said quietly. Now all eyes were on her. It was clear to Nancy that the young actress had been crying.

"Oh, yeah, a real honest mistake," David snarled.

"Just tell me, are you okay?" James asked his star directly.

"I'm fine," David insisted. "Except for that whole life-flashing-before-my-eyes thing," he added sarcastically with a last glance at George.

"Then get yourself to costume right away," James told him. "We have to begin shooting."

David seemed all too happy to get as far away from George as possible. He hurried off across the set, muttering something about needing a bodyguard.

James stepped over to Lori. She was crying softly, and her makeup was smeared. "What happened?" he asked.

"Oh, Dad. He—he was starting the same old stuff. Why did I break things off? Couldn't we get back together again? I kept saying no. And then, like last time, he decided to use his 'charm,' and he tried to kiss me."

"That's when I came in," George said, looking sheepish. "I thought he was, you know, attacking her."

"I know you were just trying to help." Lori smiled at George. "I do appreciate it."

Nancy had to fight to keep herself from laughing at the sight of George, whose hat was hanging off her head by a single bobby pin. Her narrow skirt was torn, and her stockings sagged at the ankles.

George caught Nancy's amused expression. "Thanks very much, Drew," she said, making a comic curtsy in Nancy's direction.

Susie sighed loudly. "Lori and David fight almost as much as James and I do." She leaned against the hood of a car. "And I'm getting tired of it." She moved away from the car with an irritated shake of her head and walked away.

James watched her go, then turned his attention back to Lori. "You okay, Princess?" he asked her. She nodded but avoided looking him in the eye. He smoothed a few tears from her cheek and held her face in his hands. "Okay, then get over to makeup and have your face fixed."

"I'll go with you," Nancy offered. She had a

few questions to ask Lori about David Raymond—and they weren't giddy fan questions.

As the two girls walked off, Nancy could hear James thanking George. "Don't worry about it, George. Actually, I'm glad you were there," he was saying. He sounded tired. "David has been bothering Lori ever since they broke up."

Lori smiled weakly at Nancy. "This hasn't been an easy working situation for Dad," she commented. "First, Susie's always on his back, lots of times right in front of the cast and crew. Then"—she lowered her voice—"there have been those messages. And everything going on between David and me hasn't helped."

"Tell me about David Raymond," Nancy said.

Lori sighed. "He'll never forgive me for breaking up with him. When we split up, he'd already signed the contract to do *Dangerous Loves,* so we were stuck. Things got worse when he found out how much I'm getting to make this picture. Let's just say it's a lot more than he's making. My TV career has set me up pretty well to make the transition into film."

"Do you think he's angry enough to have sent those messages, or that snake? Maybe he's trying to get the money he thinks he deserves—and more."

Lori turned her head sharply and looked at Nancy. "Oh, no! David may be a jerk, but he's not a bl—"

Nancy put a finger to her lips. She didn't want Lori to mention anything out loud.

Nancy was quiet for a moment. She could tell the actress still had feelings for David; it had been written all over her face during and after that little scene with George. Lori didn't *want* David to be the blackmailer, but that didn't mean he wasn't. Nancy decided she would have to find a way to talk to David and see what she could learn from him.

Lori and Nancy navigated through the alleys between trailers, heading for makeup. They passed a section of the set where the crew was busy preparing for the shoot. Dimly lit streetlights and drab building stoops on the set cast a somber feel and yet made it all look remarkably real. It was almost eerie, Nancy thought, as if they'd traveled through time and were strolling through another era.

Looking away from the set, Nancy noticed a man pushing a dolly with some boxes marked Special Effects Coordinator. That reminded her that she wanted an opportunity to speak with Danielle Wilner.

"Lori, could you introduce me to Danielle?"

"No problem. Let's hurry, though, so I can get over to makeup."

"Danielle's on the weird side," Lori said as they walked. "I don't know what you'll think of her. She's okay, if you like vampires, that is. But she's really good at what she does."

"What makes her so good?" Nancy asked.

"She can do anything," Lori told Nancy. "She is a *total* whiz on the computer. If it can't do what she wants it to, she invents a way to do it herself. She could have a second career as one of those millionaire microchip-heads in Silicon Valley except that she's too creative for that. But I don't think Daddy really appreciates her."

"Why not?"

"Well, naturally directors have to deal with a lot of personalities on set, but I guess Dad can't seem to get past her personal style. She has a strange sense of humor, and she's always playing weird practical jokes. I was at her apartment once when she was tutoring me for my computer class at school, and when I went to use the bathroom, a skeleton popped out of the shower at me. She'd rigged it up with a remote control."

"Charming," Nancy commented dryly.

"Yeah. But as I said, she's really a whiz. When she was tutoring me, she kept showing me all these amazing projects and ideas she was cooking up at this major home office of hers. She wasn't all that interested in tutoring me, but Dad paid her plenty for it. I guess she needs a lot of money to maintain a computer habit like hers."

"Hey, Lori," someone yelled, waving.

"You ready for the big death scene?" another crew member asked.

Lori greeted everyone, calling each crew member by name. She was obviously well liked on the set and didn't show any signs of being a prima donna, Nancy thought. Around them, the set whirled with action and movement. The pace had picked up, gaining energy and force as everyone moved closer to the moment when the cameras would roll.

Lori came up behind a woman in a long, flowing black dress bent over a huge panel of buttons and levers. A computer screen glowed on either side of her. Lori tapped the woman on the shoulder. The woman held up one finger, and when she had finished her task, she straightened up and said, "Hey."

"Danielle, this is Nancy Drew," Lori said. "Nancy, meet Danielle Wilner."

Danielle had her dyed, jet black hair pulled up in a huge, messy ponytail on the top of her head. She wore black eye makeup in pronounced circles around her eyes, and her lipstick was also black. A little gold stud glinted from the side of her nose.

Danielle held out her hand to Nancy.

As Nancy's grasp connected with Danielle's, she was startled to feel the cold, dead grasp of a cadaver. Danielle pulled her arm away, and Nancy found herself holding a severed hand dripping with blood.

Nancy stifled a disgusted shout. In a moment it was clear that the hand was made out of some highly elastic rubber, and the blood was some kind of stage concoction.

Danielle let out a nasal laugh. "Gotcha," she said. "I've been waiting to do that to someone all day." She grabbed the rubber hand back from Nancy and turned to Lori. "How you doing?" She pointed at Lori. "You look terrible. David?"

Lori nodded but said nothing about what had happened just a short while earlier. It seemed everyone knew about the uneasy relationship between the two stars. "Hey, listen, my family, uh, acquired a snake. A boa. That's what it is, right, Nancy?"

Nancy nodded.

"Oh, you're a snake lover, too? Cool." Danielle seemed to take new notice of Nancy. She turned back to Lori. "Let me guess. You want me to take the snake." She leaned against the edge of the computer console. "No problem. I had two. Now I've got one. One died just last week. And I'd love to replace him."

Her snake died? Nancy thought, raising an eyebrow. Just last week? Some coincidence. Maybe it hadn't died at all; maybe Danielle had packed it in a flower box and had had it delivered to Raye. Nancy noticed Danielle hadn't asked how the Jacksons happened to get the snake. Was it because she already knew?

"Thanks, Danielle," Lori said. "I'll make sure it gets into your car at the end of the shoot tonight. You'll love this snake. It's a biggie."

"'Bye, Danielle. It was nice to meet you," Nancy said as she headed off with Lori. But the strange woman was already hunched over her console with eyes only for her computer screens.

As she followed Lori, Nancy made a mental note. Danielle definitely was expert enough to pull off the snake stunt. Nancy was also willing to bet that, with all that high-tech know-how, she could figure out how to ferret out information on Mr. Jackson's past—that would be simple for Danielle, with her computer knowledge. Was there a motive? Money had to be the purest, most obvious motive for blackmail. I'll have to keep my eyes open, thought Nancy.

"Okay! Cameras . . . roll!" James Jackson called.

It was the big moment, the big scene of the evening. As much as she had on her mind, Nancy couldn't help but feel a little thrill of excitement. She looked over at George, and the two shared a grin.

James raised one hand above his shoulder. "And . . . action!" he shouted, dropping his hand as if to start the drivers of a drag race.

Nancy and George, along with a dozen or so other extras, sauntered in pairs or small groups down the dark street of the set. The water that rained down from the weather machine didn't actually touch them, it just slicked the pavement between them and the movie cameras. The extras pretended that they were hurrying around, avoiding rain, or huddling under their black umbrellas.

"Okay, extras, make your exit," James cried.

Slowly, the couples and small groups edged off the set. Nancy and George stepped off-camera and turned to watch the rest of the scene. At that moment Lori made her entrance. She stood for a moment in the beam of a single streetlight before beginning her walk down the street. Her long hair was wet, and she shivered. The set was actually hot under the lights, but the scene was meant to seem chilly.

Lori had an incredible charisma, Nancy decided as she and George watched from a spot offstage. The young woman she'd chatted with moments earlier had been replaced by a self-confident professional. All traces of tears and anxiety had been completely wiped away, and Lori took charge of the scene just by her presence.

From the other end of the street, David stepped onto the set. Two separate cameras would catch his expressions and Lori's, while the wide-angle cameras took in the interaction between them. David was wearing an army uniform. In his hand, a small, snub-nosed prop pistol glinted under the lights.

"Jolene!" David shouted the name of Lori's character, and waved the gun at her.

Lori looked up, startled. She took a moment to let his presence register. Then her expression dissolved into terror.

"No, Claude! No!" she cried.

David's character sneered, and then he fired. The pistol let off a *pop, pop,* a smaller, tinnier sound than Nancy expected, almost like a toy gun. White smoke escaped from the pistol's nose.

At the other end of the street, Lori let out a pained, muffled cry. Her body went limp as if she were a puppet and someone had cut the strings

43

that held her upright. She crumpled to the ground, and after a few seconds, she was still. Nancy knew the cameras were catching her every quiver.

"Cut!" James yelled. "Terrific. That was just great."

It was true. The scene was totally realistic. If she hadn't known better, Nancy would actually have believed Lori had been shot.

"Lori?" James called out as the crew began to break up. When Lori didn't answer, he called a little louder. "Princess?"

Nancy felt her mouth go dry. Something was terribly wrong.

She and James rushed over to Lori's motionless body. They saw, at the same moment, a little river of blood leaking from one of Lori's shoulders, glistening almost purple in the artificial light.

Chapter

Five

JAMES JACKSON PACED back and forth in the small hospital room. His wife, Raye, sat silently in a chair near Lori's bed, her eyes red from crying. The level of tension in the room was stretched to the breaking point, and Nancy felt slightly awkward, as if intruding upon a family drama. Between getting Lori to the hospital and dealing with the agitated members of the cast and crew on the set, none of them had gotten any sleep the night before. Lori's mother had insisted the morning be spent catching up on a bit of sleep. Still, the weariness showed on their faces, and Lori's father couldn't seem to stop pacing.

"Mom, Dad, would you please relax?" Lori said. "I'm okay. You heard the doctors." She rolled her eyes at Nancy. "It was a smoke pellet, not a real bullet."

Raye stood up and straightened the covers over her daughter. "I know," she said. "But still . . ." She gently pushed a long lock of Lori's hair off her forehead.

A nurse knocked on the door, then walked in. "Excuse me, but it's time for Ms. Jackson's medication." She handed pills to Lori in a small cup, poured her a glass of water, and stayed just long enough to be sure Lori swallowed all of them.

"We're thankful that you're okay," James said, responding to his daughter's attempt to reassure them. "But that was no accident on the set."

He looked anxious and tormented. Nancy could see that he blamed himself, for he had received another E-mail message, in which the author had taken responsibility for the shooting.

James sighed. "This psycho is stepping up the level of these threats. I mean, Lori's been *shot!*" There was an edge of panic in his voice.

It was true. Nancy hoped she hadn't gotten involved in this case too late. She felt a wave of anxiety as she thought of all she needed to do on this investigation. She wanted to spend some time talking to Lori alone about David. She needed to question the prop people on the set about the gun. And she wanted to get back to the Jacksons' home to study all the E-mail messages James had received.

For now, she'd left the task of investigating the snake delivery to George. If they were lucky, by the time they met again at the set late that afternoon, they might have come up with a clue Nancy could actually use.

Liam hurried in and out of Lori's room, gradually transforming the plain hospital room into a cozy haven. Vases of exotic flowers sat on every surface, including the windowsill. And Liam had brought in a VCR to connect to the television in Lori's room. A stack of videos littered the floor beside the TV; members of the cast and crew of *Dangerous Loves* had made a collection, each donating two or three of their favorite videos for Lori to watch while she was recovering.

James continued to pace. "I could handle it when this joker was threatening only me. But now, my family's in danger, and I've got to do something to stop it."

His wife patted his shoulder, trying to calm him. "What kind of a person would do this?" she asked no one in particular. Nancy wished she had an answer, but she had nothing much to go on yet.

"Now, remember, we have no evidence at this point," Nancy began carefully, "but we certainly can consider a few people we know who have the means or the motive."

All eyes turned to Nancy. "First, let's talk about Danielle. As special effects coordinator, she has the run of the set. She could easily have rigged the prop gun to shoot a smoke pellet instead of a blank, right? Then there's Raye's snake-in-the-box delivery, and we know Danielle has no problem handling snakes. We also all know she's a computer genius—it would be easy for her to send those untraceable E-mail messages."

James nodded. "No objections so far," he said.

"Then there's David Raymond," Nancy continued. "This is so obvious it's almost silly, but he *is* the one who actually shot Lori. The gun had been in his pocket for a short while before the cameras began filming, so he had the opportunity to replace the blank with a smoke pellet. And with Lori and David's rocky history . . ."

Lori sighed and looked out the window as dusk closed in. She turned back to Nancy with a scowl on her face.

"Has anyone ever considered that what happened last night just might be an *accident?*" Lori demanded.

She looked around the room defiantly. "I mean, really, mistakes like this are made all the time on film shoots. This wouldn't be the first time it happened, and it won't be the last."

"First of all, young lady, may I remind you that you were *shot?* 'Mistakes like this' don't happen 'all the time.' If they did, the film industry would shrivel up and die.

"Second, Nancy just mentioned the gift of our lovely boa constrictor as a door prize at our home. You're fooling yourself if you think these incidents aren't connected."

Nancy was about to add Susie Yaeger to the list when a loud knock interrupted the conversation.

"Who is it?" James called out sharply.

"It's just me, Trent," a voice offered as the door swung open and Trent popped his head inside.

Nancy was secretly glad to see the screenwriter again, and she couldn't help appreciating how good he looked in his casual sweater and slacks. But she immediately noticed that his face looked pale and anxious.

"All this hospital security! They almost didn't let me in here." He hurried over to Lori's bed and kissed her on the forehead, then presented her with a huge lily plant. "I hope you're okay," he said sincerely.

"I'm fine, Trent, thanks," Lori said with a smile. "It was just a smoke pellet—more bark than bite, really." Nancy saw James turn toward his wife and take her hand.

"Well, I'm glad to hear that. You sure know how to turn up the drama a few notches, kid. David's going to think you're trying to steal his scenes," he teased.

Then he turned to Nancy. "Hey, Nancy. Too bad your first afternoon on the set ended on such an awful note," Trent said. "Making movies is not always so stressful, I promise." He took a step closer to her, and she tried to concentrate on the freckles that dusted his cheeks.

"Luckily, Lori is going to be just fine," Nancy said. She wanted to have a good look at him— she couldn't shake the attraction she was feeling. Instead, she took the lily plant from Lori and looked around for a place to set it down. She

managed to squeeze it between two arrange-
ments on the windowsill.

"James, what a terrible accident," Trent said
sympathetically. "You sure didn't need this."

James Jackson sighed. "No one did. And least
of all, Lori." He looked at his daughter sadly.
"I'm afraid it wasn't an accident."

Nancy pressed her lips together. She wished
James hadn't said that. As far as she could tell,
no one outside this hospital room suspected that
the gun had been rigged. The director needed to
be very careful not to let on to anyone that he
was being blackmailed. Even a close friend like
Trent shouldn't know.

"What are you talking about?" Trent asked,
concerned.

"Oh, nothing," James said, catching Nancy's
look. "I'm just tired and jumpy. You can imagine
we're all operating on autopilot here at this
point. Lack of sleep and all the 'excitement,'" he
said, smiling wanly at his daughter.

Nancy saw now that nothing around this investigation was going to be clear-cut. James had
said he'd never told anyone besides Raye and
Lori about what had happened on Rapid Island.
But maybe he'd dropped a hint here or there,
mentioned just enough to tip someone off to the
incident in his past. Hollywood was a very small
world, Nancy thought. One thing was for certain,
though. Whoever was blackmailing him was on
the set; no one else could have had access to the

gun. But there were dozens—probably hundreds—of people associated with the movie.

Trent clasped James's shoulders in a gesture of comfort, then turned to the hospital bed. "Hey, Lori. How about watching a video? You've got enough to choose from." He bent down and looked through the videos on the floor. "There are some great movies here."

"No kidding. There are enough videos to keep me going for a month. Luckily, I'll be out of here in a day or so." She lifted her head a bit to peek at the stack. "Let's watch that old Charlie Chaplin comedy," Lori suggested.

Trent poked around for it. "Can't find it," he said. "Oh, here's a good one—one of my all-time favorites. How about *Me and My Rolls*? It was my second collaboration with James. Really fine work," he explained to Nancy.

"Oh, not that again, Trent! You watch that film all the time!" James Jackson exclaimed.

Trent laughed and turned to Nancy again. "They love to kid me, but it's true—I never tire of that film. I was practically a kid when I wrote the screenplay, and I'm impressed with myself all over again each time I watch it." Trent jokingly patted himself on the back, and everyone laughed.

James shook his head and looked at Trent with affection as the young man picked up the box, took out the cassette, inserted it into the machine, and pushed the Play button.

Nancy didn't let on, but she'd seen *Me and My Rolls* about a dozen times. She knew the plot by heart. It was about a master car thief out to steal a classic Rolls Royce, and there were a number of exciting car chases in it.

The film started with a long shot of a curving mountain road as seen through a car windshield.

"This was a really tough script to write," Trent commented as the opening credits rolled. "I had to do a lot of research. I learned more than I ever wanted to know about cars."

"We know, we know," moaned Lori, who'd obviously heard it all before.

Nancy settled into a chair, and Lori leaned back on her pillows as the movie started.

Mr. and Mrs. Jackson looked as if they'd rather have teeth extracted than watch a movie just then, Nancy thought. She glanced at her watch and noted that she needed to leave soon in order to get over to the set to poke around. The afternoon was closing in already, and there really wasn't any time to waste on watching a video.

Just as Nancy was about to excuse herself, the screen went blank, then was filled with snow. "Hey!" Lori exclaimed.

A moment later the picture returned, but it was no longer *Me and My Rolls*. Instead, it was a weird computer-generated animation like the kind in a video arcade game. A car appeared on the horizon and sped down the length of a slightly curved road. Without slowing down, the car approached a long, low bridge that spanned a choppy body of water. Halfway over the bridge, the car crashed through the guardrail, hit the water, and slowly sank. A few bubbles rose to the surface, and then the water was calm, with no trace of the car or any reminder of its violent disappearance.

In the next scene, a woman emerged from the water. As everyone in the room watched, agape, the figure transformed into a skeleton. The skeleton's face filled the screen and grinned.

"You'd better find ten million by Friday, James Jackson," the skeletal face said in a garbled voice, "or your ugly little story becomes big news."

Chapter

Six

JAMES JACKSON STARED as the skeleton on the television screen winked, then crumbled into dust. The snow came back for a moment, then the movie resumed. Nancy jumped out of the armchair by Lori's bed and quietly flicked off the television.

Trent looked at James. "What was *that* all about?"

Lori's father avoided Trent's eyes. "It's a very long story. But it appears someone's trying to blackmail me," he explained wearily.

Trent's eyes widened. "Over what?" he asked. "I mean, what could anyone possibly blackmail you about?"

Raye Jackson put her hands over her face, and Lori swallowed hard.

Nancy looked over at James Jackson and

caught his eye. She shook her head slightly but emphatically to warn him not to speak further.

"Oh, you don't want to know. It's complicated and it's ugly, and I don't want to talk about it right now." James closed his eyes.

"Have you called the police?" Trent asked. "Surely they could put an end to this kind of horrible stuff." He nodded his head in the direction of the television.

Nancy followed Trent's gaze and wondered if his concern was truly genuine. He had chosen the video; could he have been responsible for the sinister message it delivered?

Before James could speak, Lori said quickly, "Oh, it's just some crackpot stirring up trouble." Nancy could tell she was trying to turn the conversation away from blackmail. "Could someone please put a *real* movie on for me? No offense, Dad. It's not that *Rolls* isn't a real movie, but . . . You understand, don't you?" Lori tried to smile at her father.

"Sure, Princess," he said.

Nancy knelt down in front of the pile of cassettes as if to look for a movie for Lori. She picked up the empty box that had held *Me and My Rolls*. It appeared to be a new copy of the movie—the box was in perfect condition. But when Nancy popped the cassette out of the VCR, the tape had no label and no identifying marks at all. The blackmailer had used a blank videocassette to tape *Rolls* and dub in the menacing message. Nancy slipped the tape into her jacket pocket.

Just then there was a knock on the door, and a nurse stuck her head inside. "I'm sorry, Mr. Jackson, Ms. Brodburne, but afternoon visiting hours are over. You'll all have to leave now to give Ms. Jackson some time to rest."

"Okay," James said with a heavy sigh. "Listen, I'll see you tomorrow. You rest up now." He leaned in to give Lori a kiss on the cheek. "I'm so sorry, Princess," he whispered.

As they all gathered their things and prepared to leave, Nancy waved to Lori and promised to come by the hospital in the morning. "I need to talk to you," Nancy mouthed silently, and Lori nodded in understanding. The last thing Nancy needed was for Trent to find out she wasn't just a family friend. As it was, Nancy had a bad feeling that people were going to find out about James being blackmailed, and then the Rapid Island story would make the newspapers even *without* the blackmailer's help.

Lori's mother said she'd be back for evening visiting hours and told Lori to call if she needed anything brought from home. Then the group made its exit.

In the hallway as they left, Trent took Nancy aside for a moment. "This situation seems pretty serious," he said. "I'm worried about James. He's been so tightly wound during this shoot, and now I know why. He'd never accept my help if I offered it to him. But would you please let me know if there's anything I can do?"

He let his hand rest for an instant on Nancy's wrist. She felt the warmth of his grasp, but her instincts told her to approach Trent with caution, no matter how charming he might seem.

"Let me give you my number," Trent said. He let go of Nancy's hand, felt in his pocket for his wallet, then took it out, and gave her a card.

"I'm going over to the set now with James for a little while. I'll call you in the morning if anything comes up," she said. For James's sake, she hoped nothing would, although she would love to have an excuse to call Trent—not just to investigate the writer further, but also because she felt attracted to him.

On the set, the mood was subdued. It was clear that everyone was rattled by what had happened to Lori the evening before. As one camera grip put it to Nancy, "Everyone in this business is superstitious, and stuff like this is like a hex on a film shoot."

While James went off to monitor the scene setups for the material he would film with David later that afternoon, Nancy went to find George. She was leaning against a pile of boxes near the place where Lori had been shot.

"Hey, George. How'd you do today?" Nancy asked as she joined her friend.

"I'll tell you, Nan, all I learned about snakes is

that there are plenty of otherwise normal people out there who consider the things cuddly, cute, good companions, sympathetic listeners, you name it. Or, at the other extreme, they tell me that snake meat tastes just like chicken. Bleh! It gives me the shivers."

Nancy grinned. "But was it worth it? Did you find anything?"

George shook her head. "No leads on where our boa constrictor came from. I tried the flower delivery company, local and regional pet stores, everything I could think of. Our blackmailer covered his or her tracks like a pro. How's Lori doing?"

Nancy told George about the sinister message they'd seen in Lori's hospital room and told her she had the innocent-looking video in her pocket.

"Creepy," George said.

"No kidding. Whoever's doing this has a sick sense of humor," Nancy said, shaking off the image of it. "Anyway, let's go talk to the production crew that worked on Lori's last scene."

An hour later Nancy and George had questioned the production crew, the props assistant, even the wardrobe manager. They all repeated what they had told the police—there had been nothing unusual about the scene preparation, no unauthorized handling of props or equipment, no reason to believe the incident was anything more than an unfortunate accident. The props mistress took responsibility for not triple-checking the gun before shooting began on the scene, but it was clear she never thought she had any reason to do so, since she had checked it twice already. The last she'd seen of the gun, it was loaded with blanks and ready for use.

"Now what?" George asked.

Before Nancy could answer, she caught sight of Danielle Wilner walking briskly to her special effects office.

"George, come on," Nancy said, nodding in Danielle's direction. "Let's see if we can get our resident computer genius to 'volunteer' some information about E-mail etiquette."

Nancy and George found Danielle hunched over her computer monitors a few moments later. "Hey, Danielle," Nancy said. The dark-haired woman jumped at the sound of Nancy's voice, and instantly she cleared her computer screen before turning around to face her.

"What's up?" she asked, smiling grimly.

After introducing George, Nancy launched into her small lie. "I need some information about computers," she began. "And all sources on the set here tell us you're the local expert," she continued, hoping to appeal to Danielle's vanity.

"Yep, I know my way around the Net. What do you want to know?" Danielle asked, glancing back at her computer screen.

"Well, this is a little silly, but—I'm staying with the Jacksons, and I'm dying to send an E-mail message to my boyfriend back home."

"Yeah?" Danielle said flatly. "Any ninny can send an E-mail."

"But I want to send it anonymously. I don't want him to know it's from me. It's just a friendly little prank," Nancy said, shuffling one foot in an act of coyness.

Danielle studied Nancy for a moment. "Really," she said evenly, as if measuring Nancy's simple request. "Look, I don't have a lot of time here," she began. Then she seemed to change her mind, perhaps unable to resist showing off her knowledge. "It's a simple matter to send an untraceable E-mail. You'd just use a program that allows the sender of the E-mail message to assume a diversionary alias or that offers no trace of the E-mail's origin or the identity of the sender."

"Sounds great," Nancy said. "I'll have to look into it."

"You do that," Danielle said. "I assure you," she said slowly, as if speaking to a small child, "anybody could send an untraceable E-mail. Now, if you'll excuse me?" She lifted the fake corpse-hand, which was now sitting on her desk, in a gruesome goodbye gesture.

"Yeah, sure. Thanks, Danielle," Nancy said.

Nancy and George turned and walked away.

"Sweet woman," George said, raising her hands toward Nancy in mock-corpse fashion. "I guess giving up information about untraceable E-mail doesn't mean anything one way or another," she continued, dropping her hands to her sides.

"Yeah, but did you catch what Danielle had on her screen when we surprised her?" asked Nancy.

"No," George said. "What was it?"

"The start of an E-mail message. It was addressed to James Jackson," Nancy said.

George stopped walking and looked at Nancy. "That, in itself, doesn't prove anything, though," she said after a moment's thought. "I'm sure James Jackson gets plenty of legitimate messages every day." The girls continued walking.

"True," Nancy said. "But Danielle was very quick to insist that it didn't take a genius like her to send untraceable E-mails. I couldn't tell if she was insulting me by mildly implying I was a dummy or covering up the fact that she has the technology to do it."

"And dubbing a creepy computer message onto that video would be no problem for our pale friend, with all the equipment she has at her fingertips," George mused.

"Right," Nancy agreed. "She certainly cleared that screen in a hurry. I wish I'd seen more of what she was writing."

It didn't take much for George to convince Nancy to go home and get to bed. With all the commotion, no one had gotten much sleep the night before. The pair found James Jackson blocking a scene with David, and it was clear he still had hours of work ahead of him. James gave Nancy and George a proper introduction to David, as their earlier meeting had been uneasy at best. Then the girls bade them good night, and Liam drove them back to the Jackson mansion.

As they made their way to their rooms in the guest wing, Nancy said, "I hope we come up with some clues tomorrow."

"Wow, you *must* be tired," George said. "You're always the one who's sure there's a clue to be found in an empty room."

Nancy smiled. "You're right. It's just that there are so many people involved in making a movie, we could investigate for a month and never even come close to meeting all the people who *might* have a grudge against James. If there's one thing I'll say about Hollywood, it seems like everyone has a motive. Motives, we've got. It's hard evidence we need."

The girls vowed to renew their efforts in the morning as they said their good nights and went to their separate guest rooms.

Nancy quickly brushed her teeth, washed her face, and put on her nightshirt. Then she fell into her luxurious bed. The crisp linens felt cool against her skin, and the soft scent of potpourri hung lightly in the air. But the comfortable surroundings did little to relax her. She tried to imagine being with Ned or to conjure up some equally pleasant thought, but her mind kept returning to the image of the video skeleton disintegrating before her eyes. Finally, the late hour took its toll, and she fell into a deep sleep.

The next morning at the Jackson mansion, everyone woke early and regrouped over a breakfast of coffee, scones and muffins, and a variety of fresh-squeezed juices. As he ate, Mr. Jackson complained about not being able to join his wife at Lori's bedside. "But there's no way I can put this movie on hold," he said with a scowl.

Nancy thought about Mr. Jackson's predicament as she nibbled on a blueberry muffin. She could understand his frustration. His personal life was in turmoil, yet every hour that production was held up added thousands of dollars to the film's tab. And Susie wouldn't stand for that. It suddenly occurred to Nancy that the blackmailer was turning up the pressure at the most critical moments. Whoever it was, the person seemed to be very aware of the day-to-day progress on the film.

"So, are you two coming to the set?" James asked, glancing at Nancy and George and snapping Nancy out of her musing. He drained the last of his coffee. "We could use you as extras again."

"Absolutely," George said enthusiastically. "And I'm going to make it my mission to befriend David Raymond and make it up to him for the other day. It might surprise you to learn it's actually *not* my habit to go around kicking handsome men in the face."

They all laughed as they finished with breakfast, then walked out to the limousine Liam had pulled up to the door. The plan was for Liam to drop off Raye and Nancy at the hospital before taking James and George to the set. As Liam steered through the slow-moving, heavy freeway traffic, Nancy, who was sitting in the back, looked out the window at the other drivers.

There was a blond with her hair in a french twist driving a Jaguar. A middle-aged couple argued in the front seat of a battered four-door.

Then, abruptly, the traffic came to a halt. Behind them, a few horns honked. Beside them in the next lane, a well-dressed man sitting behind the wheel of his car picked up the newspaper beside him, obviously deciding to make the best of being stuck in traffic. Nancy sat up straight as she spied a headline on the front of the man's paper. The heading read: "Young Star Shot on Movie Set."

Nancy noticed that Raye was also looking out the window at the same newspaper. Before Nancy could say anything, Raye spoke up.

"Darling," she said to her husband, "did you read the paper this morning?"

James, who was sitting in front, shook his head. "I didn't have time. Why?"

Raye Jackson silently pointed through the glass toward the man reading the paper, and her husband groaned. "It's hard enough dealing with something like this without all the publicity. Who would leak this story? The crew was advised not to speak to the press." James rode the rest of the way to the hospital staring out the window in sullen silence.

When Liam pulled up to the front of the hospital, James jumped out and began collecting newspapers from the machines that lined the wall near the door. Nancy and Raye got out of the car and read the headlines over his shoulder.

"Lori Jackson Rushed to Hospital," reported one paper. "Foul Play?" asked a tabloid over a nearly full-page photograph of Lori.

"I wonder if I'll get an E-mail message taking credit for leaking this story," James said angrily. "Next time I'm sure we'll all be reading about Rapid Island." His tone was bitter. "Well, so much for keeping this story quiet." He shook his head. "I'd better talk to Susie. She's not going to like it. This kind of negative publicity could kill the film. We're going to have to do some major damage control."

James kissed his wife, then dashed back into the car. He rolled down the window and called to Nancy, "I'll send Liam back for you in an hour. Meet me at my trailer at eleven o'clock." Then the limousine sped off, with James and George in the backseat.

"I'm so worried about James," Raye said as she and Nancy entered the hospital. "I've never seen him so stressed out. I'm beginning to think he should come out in the open with the Rapid Island story before he collapses from the tension."

"If he did that, we might never find out who's been trying to blackmail him. And the studio would probably drop him from the film," Nancy said quietly.

"I know all that," Raye said impatiently. "I don't care about the money. I'm worried about my husband, my daughter, the life we've worked so hard to make here."

Nancy touched the woman's arm. "I'm sure you're a great comfort to James through all of this."

"Thank you, Nancy. Sometimes it's just so difficult maintaining some measure of calm. But I need to be strong, even if I have to call upon all my acting skills to do it."

They found Lori in good spirits, sitting up with an array of glossy magazines spread across her lap and her barely touched breakfast on the table beside her bed.

"Mother, you have *got* to get me out of here. I feel like I'm in jail!" Lori complained dramatically. "Can't I lie around and recuperate in my own bed at home?"

Raye Jackson smiled at her daughter. "That's just what I wanted to discuss with your doctor this morning. Why don't you and Nancy visit while I go track him down."

Nancy settled into the chair next to Lori's bed. "So, how are you feeling?" she asked.

"I feel fine, really I do," Lori insisted. "I swear I could go back to work on the set today. But the doctor says it would be best if I rest and stay pretty still a while longer." Lori sighed. "How's my dad?"

"Not great, I'm afraid," Nancy answered. "The newspapers were filled with sensational accounts of the shooting."

"Oh, no. Dad's probably going berserk, worrying about all the crummy publicity. Susie's going to flip out." Lori frowned. "You've got to help us find out who's doing this stuff, Nancy."

"I'm trying," Nancy said. "Listen, I only have a few minutes. Tell me more about you and David Raymond."

"Only if you promise that what I tell you won't turn up in tomorrow's gossip columns!"

Nancy laughed. "I promise. Now, can you tell me more about what broke up you two?"

"David and I were very close," Lori began. "He seemed like a terrific guy, very devoted, very romantic. Our relationship became serious pretty soon after we started dating."

"Were you in love with him?" Nancy asked.

"Yeah, I mean, sure, I think so," Lori answered. "You see, that was the problem. I thought I was in love, whatever that means. Nancy, I'm eighteen years old. David's the first real boyfriend I've ever had. So I don't know much about being in love, or what love is, but I do know enough not to do anything stupid just because I *think* I'm in love."

Nancy leveled a questioning look at Lori but didn't say anything.

Lori continued. "After we had been dating for

about six months, David decided he wanted to get married. And he wasn't kidding. There he was, down on one knee, proposing to me—just like in the movies," she said. "Right then and there, I knew things had gotten a little out of control. I told him I didn't want to get married, and I told him I thought we needed to slow things down, maybe take a break from each other."

"How'd he take that suggestion?" Nancy asked.

"He didn't. He said we didn't need a break, we were fine, I was just nervous. I told him I wasn't nervous, I was leaving. Breaking up. Saying goodbye. He went crazy. He started yelling all this nutty paranoid stuff about how I was Daddy's little girl, and James Jackson probably didn't think he was good enough for his 'Princess.'"

Nancy nodded. David Raymond was beginning to move to the top of her A-list of suspects.

"I know what you're thinking, Nancy." Lori looked at Nancy pleadingly. "But you can't take all of this too seriously, and you can't confront him. Believe me, it'll only make things worse. David's just very passionate."

"Lori, more than a few crimes have been committed in the name of passion. Hollywood's full of stories, but so is real life. Just ask Claude, or whatever David's character is called in *Dangerous Loves.*"

"I'm just trying to tell you that you shouldn't

approach David about this. He plays all his parts, in life and art, to the hilt—jilted lover, angry soldier . . ."

"Psychotic blackmailer," Nancy finished her sentence.

Lori nervously plucked at the blanket of her hospital bed, seemingly struggling with some thought.

"What is it, Lori?"

"I have to tell someone," she began after a moment, as if to herself. "Nancy," she whispered, looking up. "I'm scared of him."

Chapter

Seven

A SHORT WHILE LATER, Liam dropped Nancy off at the studio. She quickly headed toward James's trailer, eager to give him the good news that Raye Jackson had told her before she left the hospital—the doctors were pleased with Lori's progress, and an early release from the hospital looked likely. She was just about to knock on the door, when she heard two familiar voices engaged in an angry exchange.

"Well," James said, "what are we going to do about all this negative publicity?"

Susie sounded amazed. "Negative publicity? Are you kidding? There is no such thing as negative publicity. This is just what we need to work up some badly needed interest in this film."

For a moment there was silence. Then James's voice grew louder and edgier. "This was a private matter concerning my daughter, not just some fluff business. We have a difference of opinion on this publicity issue, Susie."

"We sure do," Susie responded. "I couldn't have been more pleased when the papers picked up my story."

"Your story? So it was you who—"

"Yes," Susie interrupted. "I leaked the story to the press."

"Susie, I wanted this kept quiet," James snarled. "Don't you have an ounce of respect for my family's privacy?"

"I'm sorry." She didn't sound sorry at all to Nancy. "But I couldn't let a chance like this go by. This exposure is bound to increase ticket sales. And that is what we are trying to do here, isn't it?" Her voice dripped with sarcasm.

While Nancy listened outside, she noted how easily Susie had been able to get her story into the papers. It was no surprise—surely every effective producer in Hollywood knew how to bait the press. But it did make her think about Rapid Island. About how easy it would be for Susie to get that story in the papers—if she was the blackmailer.

"You are one cold person," James Jackson said. "I guess it's true what they say about you— you'd run over your grandmother to defend your bottom line."

"Hey, it's my job. To know me is to love me, it's true," she said. "But what I want to know is, is it true what they say about *you?"* With that,

Nancy heard the doorknob click, so she stepped aside as Susie Yaeger bounded down the steps of the trailer with a smirk on her face. She stormed past Nancy without even noticing her.

Nancy slipped into the trailer and found James Jackson slumped in a chair, his head buried in his hands. He looked up when he heard the door close, and Nancy saw the tiredness in his eyes.

"I just spoke to Susie," he said quietly.

"I know. I heard pretty much everything. She's a tough cookie," Nancy commented.

"You have no idea," James answered.

"James, you have to find your strength and keep going on this film. The blackmailer thinks he'll either get the money from you, or he'll drive you to ruin. Since we know the first isn't going to happen, we need to work like mad to prevent the second. We're going to stop this person, I just know it," Nancy said emphatically.

"Have you discovered something?" James asked, his voice tinged with hope.

"Nothing hard yet, but I'm beginning to get a strong feeling for my suspects. There's no time to lose, though, so let me get back to my investigation," Nancy said, giving the director's hand a squeeze.

As they left the trailer, Nancy thought that Mr. Jackson looked somewhat heartened. He was immediately enveloped by half a dozen people anxious to speak with him about the shoot. He answered them one by one, issuing orders and answering questions. Nancy marveled at the calm with which he was able to conduct himself.

Nancy spotted George and waved her over. "How's it going?" she asked, pulling her aside a few steps from the small group surrounding James.

"Pretty well. I've been nosing around a bit today. Turns out nobody, but nobody, is allowed near any of the special effects equipment except Danielle Wilner, by order of the gruesome special effects coordinator herself. On the set, anyway, she'd be the one most likely to have been able to put together a video like the creepy one you described. Who's to say it was created here on the set, though?"

"Mmmm, interesting, just the same," Nancy mused. "It had to have been done very quickly and efficiently. Someone would have to have known of the shooting, known the cast and crew was collecting video donations for Lori, and known where Lori was hospitalized."

"Yeah," George agreed. "There are a bunch of reasons why it makes sense that the video was dubbed right here, in a hurry. But there's nothing on the video itself to indicate where the work was done, unfortunately."

Nancy frowned and looked at the ground in thought.

"Hey, I've got to get over to wardrobe. Are you coming with me?" George asked Nancy.

"You go ahead," Nancy said. "I'll be there in a few minutes."

The small group around Mr. Jackson disbanded, and Nancy was just about to speak to him again, when Trent ambled up to them.

"Hey, James. I know this must be tough on you." He gestured toward the newspaper tucked under his arm. "I want to help any way I can. Just say the word."

"There *is* something you could do for me. Keep an eye out for Nancy, will you? I don't know what I'd do without her," James said, patting Nancy fondly on the arm.

She smiled. "Oh, there's no need to worry about me. I'm pretty good at taking care of myself."

"No problem," Trent said. "I'll stick right with her." He sidled up to Nancy and linked his arm through hers. "Like gum on her shoe," he added with a wink.

"Thanks," James murmured distractedly as he wandered off toward a cluster of production people.

Trent turned to Nancy. "So . . ."

"So . . ." Nancy answered, smiling. She tried to concentrate on his freckles again, but this time her trick turned against her. She blushed to find herself wondering how it might feel to kiss one of them, just one.

"Follow me," Trent said. "I want to show you something."

Glad to snap out of her fantasy, Nancy turned her attention to where Trent was taking her. They passed the trailers, then walked among crates and equipment until Trent stopped in front of a set closed off with heavy white canvas curtains.

"Here we are," Trent said. He ducked through a gap in the curtains and held one back for Nancy to follow.

Stepping inside, Nancy found herself in the middle of a perfect replica of a 1940s ice cream fountain. Round stools covered in battered red leather lined a high chrome counter. Tall milk shake machines joined rows of jars filled with licorice sticks and jelly beans and malt balls. Over long shelves of ice cream soda glasses and five-cent bottles of soft drinks, an old-fashioned sign read Two Cents Plain.

"This place is terrific!" Nancy exclaimed, whirling around to take in all the details.

Trent grinned. "I know. I love it, too."

Nancy dropped onto one of the counter stools, and Trent joined her. "I don't have a trailer of my own," Trent explained, "so unless I'm working on a new scene, I like to hang out here."

"It's a lot nicer than a trailer," Nancy noted, reaching toward one of the licorice jars. Trent took her hand, squeezed it warmly for an instant, then let go. "Hey, it's tempting, I know," he said, nodding toward the candy jars, "but remember, this is a set. If there were four licorice sticks in the jar for the first shoot, there have to be four for the second. Believe it or not, there are a few people on this set whose job it is to count the licorice sticks."

Nancy looked at him quizzically.

"Each time a scene wraps, these folks take instant photos of the set and the actors, so they can make sure every detail is just the same from one scene to the next," Trent explained. "They call it continuity."

"I'll just buy a candy bar at the vending machine," Nancy said with mock annoyance. "So, how did you get into screenwriting?" she asked.

Trent shrugged. "Well, I always loved to write, even as a little kid. My freshman year at college, I took this great history of film class, and I knew right away I'd be able to combine my two passions by writing scripts. I dropped out of school, wrote a screenplay, and moved to California. I started taking it around to studios and managed to get it produced. It was like magic, Nancy."

"It must be exciting working with James."

"Yeah, I guess it is," Trent answered.

"You don't sound very convincing," Nancy noted.

"Well, it was pretty incredible the first time, when we were making *A Taste to Die For*. I thought I was living a dream. I was sure I was about to become a millionaire." He tapped the countertop distractedly with his fingers. "But it didn't exactly work out that way."

"But that was a great film," Nancy said enthusiastically.

The movie was about a college chemistry student turned serial killer who used a variety of little-known poisons to fell his victims. Nancy remembered being impressed with the forensic accuracy of the movie. After seeing the film, she had checked the details in her well-worn reference book, *1001 Deadly Substances,* and she'd found no mistakes.

"When I first started out, I thought the experience was more important than the money," Trent said. "But I guess a guy starts to have higher hopes than that after a while. For success, you know?"

Nancy noted the regret in his voice. Just how much *does* this bother him? she wondered.

"Well, you may not be impressed with what you've accomplished, but I am. Just because the film didn't make tons of money doesn't mean it wasn't good," Nancy said.

"A few years ago I would have agreed with you, Nancy. But good reviews don't get you far in this town without ticket sales to go with them. Hey, let's change this sorry subject, shall we? Tell me about you." Trent reached for Nancy's hand.

Nancy felt a tingle. She let his hand remain on hers for the space of a delicious heartbeat. Then she gently disengaged it.

"Me? Well, I . . ."

She searched for something to say. She couldn't very well tell Trent the truth—that she was a detective investigating the threats plaguing James Jackson. And she wasn't about to start rambling on about River Heights. It wouldn't seem very exciting to a Hollywood screenwriter.

"You've got a secret of your own, don't you, Nancy?" Trent teased.

"What do you mean?" she asked.

"I have to be honest with you," he said with a sheepish smile. "When I met you yesterday, Nancy, I really liked you."

"Oh?" Nancy said with a smile, waiting for him to continue.

"So I did a little friendly research on you," Trent said.

"Trent! You checked me out?" Nancy wasn't sure whether to be flattered or bothered.

"Well, it didn't take much. James had told me you lived not too far from Chicago. After about five minutes of Web searching, I stumbled onto an article in a Chicago paper about some big mystery you'd solved. So you're a detective?" he asked.

Nancy was shocked into silence. There went her cover, totally blown. She looked hard at Trent. I sure hope I can trust him, Nancy thought. If not, James Jackson is finished.

Chapter

Eight

Listen, no one around here is supposed to know I'm a detective," Nancy said firmly. "I'm working on a very serious investigation that will be jeopardized if anyone discovers what I'm up to."

Trent seemed a little surprised by her brisk tone. "Hey, Nancy! Please don't worry. You can trust me completely. I was just trying to find out a little about you. I didn't mean to upset you."

Nancy could see he felt bad. She hadn't meant to come across so strong. "I'm sorry, Trent. I just need to know I can count on you to keep this to yourself."

"I will, I promise!" Trent said. "You're investigating the blackmail? I'll help you, just tell me what to do."

Nancy smiled. "That's okay, it's really nothing

you need to be concerned about," she said, not wanting to include him in her detective work. "You can help me most by doing what you can to keep James calm and on track with the film. He's the one I'm worried about."

"I'll do it. For you, anything." Trent took her chin gently in hand and leaned in slowly to kiss her.

Unable to resist his freckle-faced charm another minute, Nancy closed her eyes. Just then, the romantic moment was broken by the constant beeping of a horn.

Nancy jumped away from the counter and poked her head through the canvas curtains to see Lori driving up in her Maserati. She waved at cast and crew from behind the wheel.

"Hey, everyone," she called as she gingerly climbed out of her car. "The doctors wanted to release me from the hospital tomorrow, but I convinced them to let me go today. I'm all better—except for this little memento." She bared her shoulder, which was wrapped in a bandage. A small crowd formed around her, and Nancy and Trent joined them.

"I'm glad to see you're okay," Trent said. "You look terrific."

David Raymond pushed through the crowd. "Lori! Thank goodness you're all right. They wouldn't let me up to your hospital room."

There was an awkward silence until someone from the crew cracked, "Well, gee, David. Could be because you were the gunman!" Everyone laughed uneasily, even Lori.

Was David's concern real? Nancy wondered. Or was there guilt beneath it—guilt of having planned for the prop gun to misfire, of causing Lori's injury himself?

James Jackson hurried over to his daughter. "Lori, you shouldn't be here. You ought to be home."

Lori frowned. "I'm okay, Dad. Really. I want to watch you film today's scenes. I couldn't just hang around in bed all day."

Her father pinned her with a look. "I should send you home immediately." Lori's face fell. "But I won't," he relented. "Could someone get Lori a comfortable chair?"

As a young gofer hurried off to find a chair, Nancy saw David stride toward wardrobe.

"I have to run and get in costume for the crowd scene," Nancy told Trent. She touched his arm lightly and then hurried after David.

"Hey, wait up," Nancy called. David did not look pleased to see Nancy when she caught up and began walking along beside him.

"You seemed surprised to see Lori here today," Nancy said, catching her breath.

"What's that supposed to mean?" David demanded defensively.

"Nothing, I just—"

"Look, I'm sorry," David said. "I didn't mean to snap at you. I was glad to see she was okay today, that's all. You know, they wouldn't let me see her at the hospital. I've been going crazy waiting to see her, wondering how she was doing, knowing I'm the one who fired the gun. It's been terrible."

"I know. It must be very upsetting," Nancy said sympathetically.

"You don't know the half of it," David said. "I understand you're a friend of the family, so you must only know her side of it. You don't know what she's put me through, how she's strung me along, given me hope over and over again." David was walking quickly now, agitated.

"She said she wanted to marry me, and then she changed her mind without warning. She's had me in turmoil for months, and yet I know she loves me. I'm sure her father is behind our breakup, and I can't stand what he's doing to us!" David's fists clenched in anguish.

In spite of herself, Nancy found that she was beginning to feel truly sympathetic toward David. But he's given Lori reason to be afraid of him, she reminded herself. This guy's an actor, and a good one, she thought, and he might be passionate enough to do something stupid.

Aloud she said, "David, I'm sorry things have been hard for you. But you know that's not the way Lori tells the story. She says you've been acting crazy."

David stopped walking and turned abruptly to Nancy. "That's just not true. If anybody's been acting crazy, it's Lori. Now I've got to go and get ready for my next scene. I don't have anything more to say to you about this. I know what you're thinking, but I did not fire that gun to harm Lori, no matter how much she's put me through. Everybody agreed it was an accident, and if you don't believe it, I don't care."

Nancy watched David walk briskly toward his trailer. Then she went to wardrobe. George was there waiting for her, already dressed for the crowd scene.

"It's about time," she said. "I was beginning to think I was going to have to walk down the street by myself. By the way," she continued as Nancy took her outfit off a rack, "I saw Lori come on the set. She looked fine."

"I saw her, too," Nancy said. "She's doing great." She quickly took off her jeans and T-shirt. "On the way here, I had an interesting conversation with David Raymond. He was very defensive, and he assumed I thought he'd fired the smoke pellet on purpose." She quickly pulled on the 1940s skirt, then reached for the suit jacket.

"Oh, I don't think there's anything to it, Nan," George said. "I spent some time with David earlier, and he's really broken up about it all. I think he loves Lori to distraction and feels rejected."

"I wonder," Nancy mused, unconvinced. "Well, we'd better get back to the set—the crowd scene's next."

* * *

James had set Lori up in a comfortable chair on the sidelines of the area where they'd be filming. She was happily enjoying the attention of several cast members, and Nancy was glad to see that Lori truly seemed to be feeling better.

The crew had set up a street scene similar to the one they'd used when Lori had been injured. George and Nancy watched as they began lining up the vintage cars. A crowd of extras would provide hustle and bustle on the street.

Trent came over and stood beside Nancy as a director's assistant began explaining the scene to the extras. This scene was to involve a stunt in which Lori was driving along when her car radio would explode. The car would spin out of control, do a 360-degree turn, and come to a stop just inches from a brick wall.

In reality, Lori wouldn't be anywhere near the car. A stunt woman would be wearing Lori's costume so that it would appear that Lori was driving.

Nancy was confused. She whispered to Trent, "If Lori's character was shot in the scene filmed before, how is it that she's supposed to be driving around today?"

Trent smiled indulgently. "Good question," he said. "Film scenes are never shot consecutively. They're shot in whatever order saves the most time, effort, and money—and it's all figured out in advance. For example," he continued, "all scenes shot at a certain location are filmed at once, regardless of where each figures in the movie."

"That's amazing," Nancy said, impressed with the complexity of the moviemaking process.

She watched as Diana, the stuntwoman, in full costume and makeup, worked through a series of stretches on the sidelines. A crew member checked the radio, making sure it was ready to explode on cue. James Jackson studied his script, a dog-eared copy marked up with dozens of changes. He held the stubby end of a pencil, which he chewed as he read.

"Hmm," he mused almost to himself, "I'm not sure if the dialogue works here."

Nancy could see that Trent was watching the director intently. "Hey, James, I already reworked this scene twice."

James appeared not to hear him. He flipped through the pages of the script quickly, making marks in the margins.

"James, what are you doing?" Trent asked. He'd stepped over to where James was working and now peered over the director's shoulder.

"I'm just making a few changes," he said.

"But you've made so many changes already," Trent said tensely.

The director frowned. "Please don't get defensive, Trent. You know how I work."

"But—"

"Please." James Jackson held up one hand. "I know what I'm doing."

Trent swallowed hard, not saying anything more, but he shot the director an angry look. Nancy looked on quizzically. James had talked about Trent as if they were partners in the movies they made together, but now Nancy was getting a different view of their working relationship.

Without saying a word to Nancy, Trent stormed off. Nancy noticed he didn't go far, though. She watched him sit down heavily, a short distance from the action.

Nancy could understand why James might need to make changes, improvise, not stick with the script. She'd even heard Susie demand that he make cuts and James reluctantly agree to do it. But what concerned her right now was Trent. Maybe it wasn't all hearts and smiles between the two men, after all. Nancy remembered that Trent hadn't sounded very happy about their collaboration when she'd talked to him earlier.

Nancy hated to have to consider Trent in this new light, but she had to admit that maybe he had a motive. But did he have an opportunity? Could he have slipped the rigged prop gun into David's pocket before the scene in which Lori had been shot? Would he have known how to rig the gun?

She had to check it out. She made her way over to where the props mistress was checking a few last-minute details before filming began.

Nancy tapped her on the shoulder. "Excuse me," she said. "I know we've already discussed this, but James wanted me to ask you something about the prop gun that was used the night Lori was injured." It was a white lie, but she just had to know about Trent.

"Ask away," the props mistress said.

"Tell me again: did you test the gun before the scene was shot?"

The props mistress nodded. "Of course I did. Twice. And there was nothing wrong with it."

"Did you give it to anyone before David took it?"

"Yes. Danielle checked it out after I did. But then she took it right over to David. I watched her do it. And we began filming immediately after that."

Nancy smiled and said, "Thanks." The props mistress shrugged her shoulders and went on with her work.

Nancy took a deep breath as she turned to walk back to the crowd scene. So Trent couldn't have been the one who fixed the gun.

The extras were still milling about, waiting for their call. Nancy wandered over to peer at a half-completed set being built nearby. Suddenly she heard a hard-edged and authoritative voice—Susie Yaeger's.

"I'm telling you, all kinds of strange things are happening around here. I can practically predict there'll be another accident," the producer said, shutting her cellular phone with a click a moment later.

Nancy peeked around the plywood wall where she'd heard Susie, and the producer looked up at her with an annoyed look. "May I help you?" she snapped.

Nancy considered what she'd overheard. Had something else happened on the set? Was Susie reporting it to the newspapers—again?

Susie said she had let the papers in on the news of Lori's accident because publicity—any kind of publicity—was good for the movie.

But maybe there was a second reason. Maybe she hated James Jackson and blamed him for the death of her friend Bianca. Leaking to the papers hints of problems with James's film would definitely hurt him.

"Well? Were you going to ask me something?" Susie asked Nancy.

Nancy bit her lip. "No, I—I'm sorry, I'm wanted on the set," Nancy said, glad to be free of Susie's angry glare.

Back on the set, James was already calling for Nancy when she got there. "Where've you been?" he asked. "I needed you. Listen, I've made a few adjustments in this scene. You're going to like this." He held up the script; it was covered with pencil changes. "I don't think Lori's character should be in the car alone. You're perfect for the part, Nancy. Diana's a first-rate driver; you'll be perfectly safe. The car radio explosion is minor, really. It's meant to startle the driver, not cause any damage. There'll be smoke but no fire. As far as being in the car, there's no danger. It's just a little high-speed driving—I'm sure you're no stranger to *that,*" he said with a smile.

Nancy grinned. "Great." She turned to look for George, wanting to share her exciting news. She could see her in the crowd of extras, and she gave her a thumbs-up sign.

Mr. Jackson explained the scene step by step to Nancy. "So, can you do it?" he asked.

Nancy swallowed hard but grinned confidently. "Sure."

"Good, let's go."

A make-up person came over and gave Nancy's face a few extra touches of color. A hair stylist arranged her hair while James introduced her to Diana, the stunt driver. He told her once more exactly what she needed to do in the scene and when to do it. Nancy noted that James's firm, encouraging directing style would give any actor all the confidence and inspiration required. A dolly with a camera had been set up to ride alongside the car.

When every detail had been confirmed, Nancy stepped over to the car.

"You ready?" the stunt driver asked. Nancy nodded excitedly. "Okay, let's do it!"

Nancy slid into the passenger seat of the car and buckled herself in with a special seat belt.

The safety belts weren't like anything Nancy had ever seen before. They were more like the harness a sky diver would wear. They were designed to secure the driver and passengers while being hidden from the view of the camera.

Diana took the driver's seat, strapped herself in, and turned the key in the ignition. She flipped back the hair of the wig she was wearing to resemble Lori's hair, shifted the car into gear, and took off, quickly gaining speed. Extras strolled by on the street, doing their best to act naturally but seemingly surprised as the car sped by. On one side, the crew gathered to watch the scene. On the other, a brick wall hemmed in the car. One wrong flick of the wheel and Diana would send them smashing into it. The wall was L-shaped, leaving no room for escape. Just after the radio was to explode, Diana would have to spin the car in a circle to avoid hitting the wall and then instantly stop.

The car's speed increased. On cue, Nancy turned on the radio, and it appeared to explode. She braced herself as Diana prepared to swerve and maneuver the car into a spin. But the car didn't turn.

"The steering wheel is locked," Diana said with professional calm. She hit the brakes, but the car didn't slow down. "The brakes aren't working," she said in the same tone.

Nancy tried to remain calm, too. She'd been in plenty of tricky situations in cars before, she reminded herself, even in her own.

The brick wall became a blur on one side of Nancy. She watched in horror as the panicked crowd on the other side of the road began to run, everyone trying to get out of the way of the speeding car that was heading right for them.

Chapter

Nine

As THE CAR CAREENED toward the running crowd, Nancy looked over at the stuntwoman. They couldn't let the car crash into the crowd. She leaned over and grabbed the wheel, adding her weight to Diana's. The two of them tried desperately to shift the wheel.

"The wall!" the stuntwoman shouted. "Aim for the wall."

Nancy knew what she meant. The brick wall blocked them on one side and in front, but hitting that would be better than plowing into the frantic crowd of people, who were trying to scatter but could find no escape.

Nancy and Diana used all their strength to edge the car toward the wall. Diana sweated and Nancy strained. With their combined effort, the steering wheel began to give in tiny increments.

They were turning the car! It now faced away from the crowd, but the brick wall loomed.

Nancy closed her eyes and braced herself as the car hit and the wall tumbled. She opened her eyes to discover that she was alive. Styrofoam bricks bounced off the roof of the car.

"Of course," Nancy murmured. "It's a movie."

The car's momentum broke, and beyond them lay an open stretch of blacktop. Diana pulled the emergency brake, and the car jerked to a stop.

"We did it. No harm done," Diana said with a huge sigh as she unbuckled her harness.

"That's an understatement," Nancy responded. She looked down at her hands and saw they were white. "But you're right. We did it."

Within moments a crowd swarmed around the car.

Nancy felt the thrill of narrow escape, but she also felt silly for not realizing the wall was fake. They climbed out of the car, and Diana walked around to Nancy. She put her hand on Nancy's shoulder. "Girl, you kept your head amazingly well in there."

Nancy smiled. "Thanks," she said.

Diana went on. "You're strong and level-headed. I think there might be a future for you in stunt work."

That's just what I need, Nancy thought, to trade in one dangerous profession for another.

James came rushing over. "Nancy, Diana, are

you okay? I thought you were going to slam into all those people."

"So did we," Nancy answered.

"Well, thank goodness you're all right!" he exclaimed. "I'm sorry, Nancy. I should never have asked you to do that scene. What was I thinking? Your father would never forgive me if . . ." James Jackson's voice trailed off.

"Listen, James, don't worry about it. I'm fine. But you'll understand if I don't volunteer to reshoot the scene, right?" she joked.

Diana laughed, but Nancy saw that James Jackson's expression was sober. He turned, scanning the crowd of crew members and actors. "This has to stop," he murmured. Nancy knew he must be blaming himself, thinking that now he was endangering everyone on the *Dangerous Loves* set.

"I have to talk to Susie about this," he told Nancy. He marched off in the direction of the producer. Nancy followed.

Susie was leaning against a streetlamp prop, her arms crossed in front of her. She shook her head at James, as if in disgust, as he hurried up to her.

"Okay, that's it," he said to Susie quietly, but there was determination on his face. "Another 'accident.' We must postpone shooting until we put an end to this nonsense."

Susie responded calmly, too, but there was fire in her eyes. "We can't do that. I won't authorize it. And you'll be breaking your contract if you do it without my okay. We have to stick to the schedule."

James Jackson shook his head. "I understand your budget problems, Susie, but there are other things at stake here. The tension on this set is so thick that if you dropped a match, you could set it on fire. The actors can't act in this climate. I can't direct. Even the stunt people can't drive." He glared at Susie.

"Honestly, this is pathetic. You're all professionals," Susie said. "Take a break, calm down. Then get back to work." She tried to turn on her heel to leave, but James grabbed her by the arm.

"Nope, not this time," he said. "We're postponing shooting. Period. No discussion. If you want to continue making this movie today, find another director." He put his hands on his hips defiantly.

Susie looked shocked. Then she sneered. "You're quitting?"

People began to gather around, staring at the producer and the director as they argued. Even Nancy knew an argument like this would make the trade papers without anybody even trying.

"If you force me to continue after everything that's happened, yes, I'm quitting," James Jackson said.

"No," Susie said. "Do you know how much time we'd lose looking for another director?"

"I'm glad my artistic vision is so important to

you," James said dryly. He turned to the crowd and waved his hand. "That's it, folks. We're packing it up."

Susie raised her arm, wanting to appear in control of the situation. Nancy expected her to order everyone back to their places. Instead, she surprised her and said, "James is right. There's been a lot of excitement around here today. You can all have the rest of the day off, but we'll see you tomorrow, bright and early, on the set."

Nancy noticed that James looked as though he was about to protest but then changed his mind.

"Okay," he said. "We'll reconvene tomorrow. But today we rest." He smiled slightly to himself. He'd won, Nancy thought—for now.

The crowd eased away in small groups, buzzing about the car excitement, the power play between the director and producer, Lori's return to the set, and the future of *Dangerous Loves*.

Nancy headed for the crash car. She wanted to get a good look at it. The accident had to have been set up. But who did it? And how could she prove it?

She walked over to the hood and popped the latch. Peering at the engine, she couldn't tell if anything had been tampered with without fiddling around and testing some parts. But the engine was still too hot to touch. She slammed the hood.

Then she looked under the car and saw a few drops of liquid. Well, that accounted for the brakes, she thought. The brake fluid had leaked. Had someone deliberately caused it?

"Looking for something?" a voice said.

Nancy jumped.

"Sorry," Trent said. "I didn't mean to startle you."

"Oh, it's you," Nancy said with a smile.

He put his arm around Nancy's shoulder and gave her a gentle squeeze. "I'm glad you're all right," he said. "What are you doing anyway?"

"Checking out the car. I want to give it another little test drive."

Trent's eyes opened wide. "Nancy, it almost killed you once. Why would you want to try it again?"

"This is my job," she explained simply.

Trent held her arm. "Please, Nancy, don't."

"Trent, I have to test this car." She shook out of his grip. "I'm not going to give it much gas when the only brake is the emergency brake. But I want to test out the steering mechanism."

Trent ran around to the driver's side. "Okay, then let me do it." He opened the door and got in.

"Trent!" Nancy cried, exasperated.

"I'm worried about you. I care about you. And I want you to be safe," Trent said from the front seat. "So get in."

Nancy caught her breath. Part of her was insulted that Trent didn't think she could take care of herself, and another part was pleased that he was so concerned about her.

"Okay," Nancy agreed as she strapped herself in. "Just give it a *tiny* bit of gas to see if you can steer."

Diana had left the keys in the ignition, so Trent turned over the engine and shifted into first gear. The car inched forward. Trent turned the steering wheel carefully. The car responded. He turned the wheel again. It moved easily.

"The steering seems fine now," Trent said with a shrug. "Should we get a mechanic to look at it?"

"I'm sure James has already taken care of it," she said. "Even though the steering wheel seems to be okay, the brakes will still have to be checked out."

Why was the steering working now? Could this have been the first *real* accident amid all the other staged ones? But what about the leaking brake fluid?

Something was bothering Nancy. Since the near-accident with Diana, she hadn't been able to forget Susie's phone call, the one in which she had spoken to someone about "strange things" happening on the set.

If Susie was so eager to keep the film on schedule and in budget range, why was she stirring up rumors with the press or whomever else she might have been speaking to? Nancy wondered. She kept provoking James to dangerous levels of anger and frustration, doing almost as much to threaten the film's progress as the shooting and the car incident had done. Had

Susie known that something would go wrong with the car—*before* it actually happened?

It was a shocking notion, but it might make sense. If the producer was truly desperate for publicity, she just might sabotage her own film. Nancy had no reason to believe that Susie knew about the role James had played in the death of Bianca on Rapid Island. But *this* motive fit in place like a piece in a jigsaw puzzle.

So what about the gun? Susie hadn't been one of the people who'd handled it. Was she working with someone—David, Danielle, or even the props mistress?

Nancy waved her hand at Trent. "Thanks a lot for your help," she said absently.

"Could I help you with anything else?" Trent asked.

Nancy shook her head. "No, but thanks. I have to run. I'll call you, okay?" She'd just seen Susie heading for the parking lot. If Nancy didn't catch up with her right away, she'd lose her chance to confront her until the next day.

"Hey," Trent called. "Can I see you later?"

"Not sure," she called back over her shoulder. She didn't have a spare second, as Susie was already far ahead of her.

Nancy rushed to catch up with Susie in the parking lot. On the way, she noticed Lori and David Raymond standing near David's convertible. Nancy was surprised to see that they weren't fighting for once.

While Susie fussed with her keys at the door of

her car, Nancy broke into a jog to catch up with her.

"Ms. Yaeger," Nancy called out, reaching the producer at last.

"Yes?" Susie turned to face Nancy.

"I happened to hear you on the phone earlier."

Susie's expression soured. "Yes, I remember." She rubbed her temples with her middle fingers.

"Ms. Yaeger, why were you telling the newspapers about the car crash?"

A puzzled look crossed Susie's face. "The crash? What do you mean?"

"You said something about 'another accident.'"

First, Susie seemed confused. Then, she gave Nancy a wary look. "What were you doing, spying on me?"

Ugh, Nancy thought. This is exactly what I hoped wouldn't happen.

"That was no newspaper, and I wasn't talking about your accident," Susie went on angrily, before Nancy could answer. "If you must know, I was calling my husband. We hired a new house-keeper last week, and it's been one disaster after another. This morning, she broke one of my crystal candlestick holders. *That's* what I was talking about, as if it's any of your business. Who *are* you, anyway?"

"I met you the other day." Nancy knew Susie hadn't even noticed when James introduced her. "My dad's an old friend of Mr. Jackson. I'm staying with the Jacksons for a while."

Susie stared at Nancy impatiently. "Well, that doesn't explain why you're listening in on my conversations and asking me nosy questions. I have to get back to my office now to catch up on my calls. For your information," she added snidely. The producer climbed into her car, slammed the door, and drove off.

Well, that was a mistake, Nancy thought. She'd wanted to shock Susie into possibly revealing something. But she hadn't gotten anything but a lame explanation, and she'd tipped the producer off to the fact that she was being watched. Totally counterproductive. Her cover was blown with one person on the set already, and now she'd raised the suspicions of another.

Nancy walked across the nearly empty parking lot. Lori's Maserati gleamed under the late-afternoon California sun. Nancy noticed a half-dozen or so other cars. Everyone else had already left.

Well, she wasn't about to go home to watch soap operas, Nancy thought. Everyone else might have the day off, but she still had to solve this mystery. She decided to find George to see if they could hitch a ride home with Lori.

Nancy made her way to Lori's trailer. She knocked at the door, but there was no answer. She turned the handle and was surprised to find the door unlocked. No one was looking. When she was certain she was alone, she slipped inside.

The trailer was strewn with costumes, cosmetics, and magazines. A large mirror took up most of one wall. In front of it was a large dressing table covered with tubes of lipstick, eye pencils, various shades of makeup, and blush—the actress's toolbox. A clock shaped like Elvis hung over the door, his hips swiveling back and forth and making a tick-tock sound. The digital minute number on his guitar flicked from 4:03 to 4:04.

Nancy wasn't sure what she was looking for, but maybe if she snooped around a bit, she'd find some new leads. She picked up Lori's script, which was on the dressing table. It was open to the final scene of the movie, where David's character had tied up Jolene, Lori's character, in a complicated series of knots. After skimming a few pages, Nancy dropped the script back onto the messy pile of papers.

She went to Lori's closet and took out a fancy dress. It wasn't a costume; it was a contemporary dress made of black silk. Nancy couldn't resist. She held it up to herself and studied her image in the mirror. Wow, it was glamorous *and* gorgeous. Ned would approve, she thought. She put the dress back in the closet, then moved to the makeup table again. She picked up a lipstick and twisted its base. A burgundy color rose out of the tube.

Nancy felt as if she was playacting. She touched the tip of the lipstick, then put it to her mouth, and spread it across her lips. That's a funny smell, she thought. And it had a funny taste, like cottage cheese that had been sitting in the refrigerator too long.

Oh, no, Nancy realized too late. She looked around frantically for a tissue to wipe off the lipstick.

But she couldn't find one. Not with the room spinning in circles as it was. Come on, Drew, *come on!*

But it was too late for tissues. She wiped desperately at her mouth with the back of her hand. By now, her skin was smeared with lipstick, and things were getting hazy.

Moments later Nancy blacked out.

Chapter
Ten

THE RHYTHMIC SOUND of tires on pavement was the first thing Nancy heard as she gradually awoke. She felt as if her head were filled with cotton candy. As she forced her eyes open, she became aware of something rough rubbing against her wrists. Rope, she realized as her head began to clear a bit. Her hands and feet were tied up tightly, and there was something soft in her mouth—a gag, securely tied. It was dark, but she could tell she was in the trunk of a car.

Oh, great, she thought. I hope George starts to wonder where I am. She's the only one who even knows I stayed on the set today. They won't have a clue where to start looking for me—wherever I am.

The wheels bumped along on the road beneath

her. Nancy realized she had been poisoned but that Lori was clearly the intended victim. If she had walked into that trailer, Nancy thought, she'd be the one in the trunk of a car right now.

Nancy struggled against the ropes, but they refused to give. From the faint smell of leather and the relatively smooth ride, she guessed she was in some kind of expensive European sports car.

Whoever was driving this car—presumably the person who had poisoned Lori's lipstick—was swerving, and cutting in and out of traffic. Nancy heard a few horns. She could also hear the faint sound of the radio, which was tuned to a familiar song. "I want to be free. Don't you try and tie me," the lead singer wailed along with an acoustic guitar.

"I want to be free."

Tell me about it, she thought.

She considered her chances. She was tied up and gagged. If the driver of the car wanted to kill her, she wouldn't be able to put up much of a fight. For a moment she considered kicking wildly against the trunk, but she didn't really want to alert the driver to the fact that she was conscious. She tried to prepare herself for the moment when the car would stop and the trunk would open to reveal her kidnapper.

"This is KPOP, L.A.'s favorite radio station," the announcer's voice said brightly. "It's four fifty-seven on this smoggy California Wednesday. I'm Joey Joelson, bringing you today's top tunes." It was awful hearing the deejay talk as if it were just any other day, Nancy thought, as if she didn't happen to be locked in a trunk, helplessly awaiting her fate.

After a while, she felt the car veer off the road. The brakes squealed, and the car stopped.

This is it, Nancy thought. The driver switched off the ignition, and Nancy could hear the sound of the front door opening and closing.

Nancy's eyes were open wide, her fists were clenched with tension. Thirty seconds passed. Then another thirty, and the trunk lid stayed closed. Nancy heard another car door slam shut, then an engine start up, and a car peel out.

She understood in a flash. Her kidnapper was driving away, leaving her in the trunk of a car by the side of a road, with no way out. Maybe her captor intended to come back for her later. Maybe ransom would be demanded for her release. Or maybe she'd just be left there.

Nancy lay still in the darkness for what seemed like hours. A tiny sliver of fading light near the trunk's lock made her realize it was almost dusk.

As the day waned, Nancy's stomach grumbled. She hadn't eaten a thing since breakfast at the Jacksons' home, which seemed like a long time ago, and who knew how many miles away.

She struggled with the ropes, but whoever had

tied them was a master. They were tight but not so much so that they completely cut off the circulation in her hands. And the ropes were strong. Nancy knew there was no chance of slipping out of them.

As the sun went down, so did the temperature. Nancy was suddenly cold, shivering, in the costume she was still wearing from her work on the set earlier in the day. She wondered how long she could remain in the trunk before the oxygen was used up.

I need to stay calm, she thought. George will begin to wonder what happened to me. But how would anyone guess that this is where I am—in the trunk of a car, on the side of some road, somewhere. Where?

To keep her mind off her mounting anxiety, Nancy mentally reviewed the case. First, there'd been the snake, followed by the malfunctioning prop gun and the defective steering and brake mechanisms of the car. Then there had been the poisoned lipstick and the kidnapping. On top of all this, the blackmailer had a real facility with computers. This person must be a jack-of-all-trades, Nancy thought.

Who was responsible for all this? Nancy couldn't stop thinking of Susie. Was this kidnapping just one more "accident," one more unfortunate event she'd be calling in to the newspapers the next morning? So far, it did seem as though Susie had the best reason for wanting to cause trouble on the set. She'd admitted that *any* publicity, even bad publicity, was good for the film and that she'd do anything to ensure the film's success. And if she'd linked Bianca's death with James, it wouldn't be surprising if she wanted to avenge her friend's death.

But it was too soon to rule out Danielle or David, Nancy thought. Or even, she supposed, Trent.

By now the light was gone, and night had descended. Nancy, stiff and too tired even to think clearly anymore, wondered if anyone would notice the car abandoned on the side of the road.

Then she heard voices, sounding muffled from her vantage point inside the trunk. "Hey, check that out," she thought she heard.

"Too much!"

The car! Were they talking about the car?

"I'd love to give that machine a test drive," another voice said.

"Why not? There's no one around."

"Take the car? I don't know . . ."

"Come on, Woody, the thing's wide open!"

She heard doors open, and the car rocked as bodies piled in.

Adrenaline pumped through Nancy's veins, and she could feel her breathing growing shallow and rapid. They didn't know she was in the trunk. What would they do when they found her? She wouldn't have much recourse, in her condition. But she didn't have any choice, either.

Nancy began to rock back and forth, kicking the inside of the trunk as hard as possible and making as much commotion as she could.

She heard some muttering and fiddling inside the car. Then suddenly the trunk latch clicked, and the lid popped open.

Chapter

Eleven

Nancy looked out to see a young man peering in at her. He was dressed in jeans and a stained sweatshirt. When he saw her lying there, his mouth curved into a little round O of surprise. "Hey, guys! There's somebody in here," he shouted.

Nancy strained to lift her head and stared at him. Two other boys appeared, their faces backlit by the stars and moonlight. "Somebody tied her up and left her here." Nancy blinked, unable to speak because of the gag.

The first teen leaned in and reached toward Nancy. She pulled back away from his hand. Her heart was pounding so loud she couldn't hear herself think.

"Hey, don't worry," the young man softly said as he removed the gag from Nancy's mouth.

When she saw that he looked as scared as she felt, Nancy began to relax.

She inhaled, deeply and quickly, her first fresh breaths in hours. "Thanks," she whispered, her voice weak.

The boy tugged at the ropes, with no luck, so he pulled out a pocketknife and began cutting through the cord.

"I'm Joe," he said. "This is Woody and Hal." He pointed at his friends, then went back to working at the ropes. "I've never been more surprised by anything in my life, seeing you there in that trunk. It was unreal! You're real lucky we came along, you know. Who knows when—or if—anyone would have found you."

"I'm just glad we didn't find you dead. That would have really ruined our night," Hal said, joking.

"Yeah, mine, too," Nancy said with a small laugh. "I'm really grateful. Thank you."

"What happened, anyway? Who did this to you?" Joe asked.

Nancy shook her head. "I don't know." Yet, she thought.

After Joe had finished sawing through the ropes and released her, Nancy rubbed her wrists and ankles. Then the boys helped her climb carefully out of the trunk, and she stretched painfully until she'd loosened up enough to walk. She looked around and realized she wasn't far from a residential neighborhood, but the car had been left at the end of an aqueduct overpass, not easily seen from the homes above.

For the first time, Nancy got a good look at the car. It was a red Maserati with license plates that said LORI-1. Obviously it was Lori's car, she thought.

"Can we give you a lift home?" Joe asked. "We were just out riding around. We weren't going to steal the wheels or anything." He waved at a pickup truck parked across the street.

"Joe's too chicken to steal a car," Hal teased. "Nah, stealing's not really our speed," he admitted.

Nancy would have loved just to get in the truck and get out of there, but she didn't want to leave Lori's car by the side of the road.

"Thanks, but no thanks," Nancy told her rescuers. "I appreciate all your help, but I have to get someone out here to pick up this car."

She walked gingerly around to the front of the car and poked her head into the driver's open window, looking for Lori's car phone.

She picked up the phone and dialed the Jacksons' number. It rang four times. Come on, Nancy thought. Answer. On the sixth ring, James Jackson picked up. "Hello?"

"James, it's me. Nancy."

"Nancy, thank goodness. Where are you?" James sounded panicked.

"I'm not sure where I am, but I need a ride home."

"Another message came in on my E-mail. The

blackmailer took responsibility for the car crash this afternoon, then said you'd been kidnapped. Are you all right?"

"I'm fine, thanks to some guys who helped me out," Nancy responded. But it could have turned out much differently, she thought.

"Where are you? We're coming to get you," Mr. Jackson said.

"Please," Nancy said, "just send George. And Trent," she added impulsively.

"Fine," James said. "Just tell me where you are."

Nancy handed Joe the phone and he gave Mr. Jackson directions. Then Nancy asked James to give George an extra set of keys to Lori's car.

Joe, Hal, and Woody waited with her until James Jackson's green sedan pulled up with George behind the wheel and Trent in the passenger seat.

"Nancy, I'm so glad to see you!" George exclaimed through her open window. She brought the car to a halt and jumped out. She rushed over to Nancy and pulled her into a hug.

Trent was stunned. "How could this have happened?"

Joe came over. "If you're okay now, we'll get going."

"I can't thank you enough," Nancy said. She waved goodbye to the guys as they boisterously jumped into their truck and roared off. She figured they'd enjoy having a brush-with-kidnapping story to tell all their friends.

"Let's get out of here," Trent said, putting an arm around Nancy. "This whole thing is just too horrible."

"You guys take Lori's car," George said, tossing the extra set of keys to Nancy. "I'll drive James's car."

Nancy looked from the keys toward the Maserati. A few days ago, she would have jumped at the chance to take Lori's car for a ride. But she'd had just about enough of that car.

"You take the Maserati," Nancy said, tossing the keys back to George.

"Really?" George asked, incredulous.

Nancy nodded.

George grinned and held up the keys. "Okay!" She got in the Maserati and lost no time in revving the engine.

Nancy took Trent's arm and steered him toward the sedan. "You drive," she told him. "I've had it with this day."

Trent got behind the wheel and started the car as Nancy lay back against the upholstery. She closed her eyes.

"Nancy," Trent said, "this is unreal. I've been working on films for years, and nothing even remotely like this has ever happened before."

"Mmm," Nancy murmured, finally relaxing.

"How about—will you let me take you to dinner? You could use a little pampering."

Was Trent asking her on a date? For an instant, a rush of excitement replaced the weariness that weighed down Nancy's body. But then the exhaustion took over again.

"That's very sweet of you," she answered, "but I'm incredibly tired." And she was thinking of Ned. It would be so nice to curl up in his arms right now and take a vacation from all the stress. But Ned was half a continent away.

"How about just a quick bite, then?" Trent offered. "I can take you to a joint a lot of industry folks hang out at. It's good, and they're used to serving people who . . . well, who look like film people," he said, glancing at Nancy's disheveled costume.

Nancy laughed weakly as she smoothed her hair. "That'd be great, Trent. Actually, I *am* starving."

Trent pulled up to an intersection just as the light was changing from yellow to red. He pressed on the brake and shifted in his seat, turning to face Nancy. "When James received the blackmailer's message today, we were all so worried. Especially me." He stared into her eyes.

For a moment, Nancy felt hypnotized. He leaned closer. He's going to kiss me, Nancy thought. She felt confused. Did she want Trent to kiss her or not? She didn't have time to answer her own question. In the next instant, his lips were against hers. His kiss was warm and gentle, as sweet as she had imagined.

Behind them, horns started honking. The light had turned green.

Trent broke away. "Oops," he said. There was a happy grin on his face.

Before long, Trent pulled into the parking area of a chic-looking restaurant, parked the car, and helped Nancy out. Inside, Nancy phoned the Jacksons to let them know they'd stopped for something to eat. Then she joined Trent at a cozy booth.

Nancy was glad their earlier kiss had been interrupted. She didn't want to let herself get carried away. As attracted as she was to Trent, she hated the idea of being untrue to Ned. She and Trent were both quiet as they perused the menu, each lost in thought.

Soon after they ordered, the waiter brought their dinners to the table. Nancy felt she'd never been so hungry in her life and was grateful to Trent for thinking of her needs.

"This is absolutely delicious," Nancy said appreciatively. Trent reached over and playfully took a forkful of her pasta.

"Mmm, this *is* good," he agreed. "Try mine," he said, offering her a bite of salmon."

After she'd satisfied her hunger somewhat, Nancy sat back and said, "Trent, you seemed really upset with James this afternoon on the set. Does he often change your writing drastically?"

Trent set down his fork. "Yes, he does," he said slowly. "But it's all part of being a screenwriter, I guess. A screenplay goes under the hatchet of so many people—everybody involved with the film has an opinion. It's the nature of the work to be at the mercy of the producer, the director—even the actors have something to say, especially if they don't like the dialogue.

"But mostly it's the director whose pen strikes the most blows to a writer's screenplay. And to his ego," he added. "I'd be a liar if I said it didn't bother me," he finished, frowning down at his plate. Then he picked up his fork and forced a smile. "But James and Raye have been wonderful to me ever since I moved to the West Coast. I'd be a real jerk if I was ungrateful, wouldn't I?"

Nancy started to reply when she noticed a couple across the room rise from their booth, preparing to leave.

"That's interesting," she said. "Susie Yaeger and David Raymond just finished having dinner together."

As Susie neared their booth, she suddenly caught sight of Nancy and Trent. She couldn't mask the surprise on her face, and she stopped for a moment, startled.

"Ms. Nancy Drew," she said, quickly recovering and obviously having no difficulty remembering Nancy this time. "I see you're still in costume. Taking our little role a bit too seriously, aren't we?" she said snidely.

David Raymond stood beside Susie. "Hi, Nancy, Trent," he said.

Nancy rested her fork on her plate. "Yes, just finishing up a long day, and I haven't found the time to freshen up," she said, looking pointedly at Susie. "And you? I didn't know you two were dining companions."

"It's perfectly natural for a producer to treat her star to a little dinner, especially when things on the set have been so uneasy," Susie said quickly. "You tell El Director he's shaking up the talent with all the trouble he's drawing on the set. Bad luck follows James Jackson," she added.

Susie took David's arm. "Let's go, David. I'll drop you off on my way back to my office. Looks like another late night on the computer for me," she said as she and David walked out of the restaurant.

Trent reached over and covered Nancy's hand with his own. "Everything okay?" he asked.

Nancy looked at her date, wondering how much she should take him into her confidence. "Curious, seeing Susie and David here, that's all," she said. "Do you mind taking me home now?" she asked.

"Sure thing, Nancy," Trent said. "You must be one exhausted extra."

Trent paid the bill and walked Nancy to the passenger side of the sedan. A few minutes later, he pulled onto the closest freeway entry and accelerated toward the Jacksons' home.

Trent all but carried Nancy from the car into the mansion. His attention embarrassed her.

Mr. and Mrs. Jackson, Lori, and George came running. "You're okay, aren't you?" Lori took Nancy by the hand.

"We were all so worried," Raye added.

Nancy held up her hand. "I'm fine. Please don't make a fuss."

"Of course we will," James insisted.

"Nancy, if it hadn't been for you, it could have been *me* tied up in that car," Lori said.

"I've been through worse," Nancy said, which was true.

After Trent left and everyone had finished hearing Nancy's story, she drew James aside. "I need to talk to you," she said.

He motioned her into a cozy TV room where they could be alone. "I think I'm finally making some progress with my investigation," she said.

"Tell me everything."

Nancy made herself comfortable on one of the black leather couches that faced a huge television screen. "Being tied up in Lori's car wasn't pleasant, but I had time to think hard about the blackmailer. This person has to have a broad range of knowledge, as well as full access to the inner workings on the film set."

"So who do you think it is?"

Nancy didn't answer immediately. "I can't say for sure yet. Let me follow up on a few other clues first."

"Okay. But, Nancy, you're not planning to continue working on this case tonight, are you?"

Nancy shrugged. "Why not?"

James frowned. "Because you've just been drugged and kidnapped, that's why!" He shook his head and sighed. "Now, it's very late," he said. "Please go upstairs and get some rest. I promised your father I'd take care of you, and I haven't been doing a very good job so far."

Nancy was about to protest, but the fact was, she really was beat. She trudged up to her room, got undressed, and collapsed in bed.

The next morning Nancy awoke early, feeling refreshed. She took a quick shower, got dressed, then padded down to James's office and sat down at his computer. In minutes, she was cruising the Internet, hoping to stumble onto an answer to a question that had not yet fully formed in her mind.

"Hmm," Nancy thought out loud as a page came up on the screen. It listed a number of commonly prescribed knockout drugs. She printed a few pages, then moved on. She pulled up page after page of information on poisons, getting lost in her research until a knock on the door broke her concentration.

"Who is it?" she called.

The door opened, and Trent stuck his head in the room. "Hey," he said.

"Hey yourself," Nancy said with a smile. "How'd you get in here?"

"Oh, you know I'm like family around this place. I come and go as if I lived here. It's been like that since James and I first worked together," he said, stepping inside. "What're you up to?"

Nancy indicated the computer with a gesture. "Just surfing the Web a little."

Trent smiled and pulled up a chair. "Fun. What are you looking at?"

Nancy quickly hit a few keys and made the page she'd been looking at disappear. She didn't want Trent to know what she'd been studying. "Oh, this and that."

Trent took over the mouse, playing around. He skipped from spot to spot with agility. If she was good on the Web, Nancy thought, Trent was a whiz.

"Wow," Nancy commented. "You sure know your stuff."

He pulled himself away from the screen and smiled. "I use the Internet all the time to research my scripts. It saves hours at the library."

"I'm impressed," Nancy said. She waved her hand at the screen. "I suppose we ought to knock it off. I've been at it for a while."

Trent prepared to exit the Web browser and turn off the computer.

"Hold on," Nancy said before he could quit. "I just want to check James's E-mail to see if there are any other messages from the blackmailer. I'm sure he won't mind." There was one message.

Nancy read aloud the subject line of the message: " 'Important information on a *black* matter.' "

"It obviously has something to do with the blackmailer," she said, looking at Trent.

"We might as well do it," Nancy said with a shrug. "I could go get him, but what's the point of upsetting him until I know what the message is?"

She opened the message, which contained only an attachment. A moment later, she opened an image that slowly took form on the screen. At first Nancy couldn't make it out. Then she saw it was a drawing of a girl, with a large, thick line across her neck, as if she'd been decapitated.

Nancy gasped as the drawing finally came into full focus.

Underneath it were the words "Tell Nancy to be careful, or she might lose her head."

Chapter

Twelve

Nancy shuddered and looked at Trent. "Let's not tell James about this," she said, clicking on the mouse to get rid of the sickening image.

"Why not?" Trent asked. "This whole situation is getting more threatening by the minute. This is something he'd want to know about."

"I agree," Nancy said. "But he has too much to worry about already. He really is at the breaking point. And telling him now won't get me any closer to solving this case."

An anxious expression crossed Trent's face. "But James deserves to know about this. I really feel we have a responsibility to tell him."

"Even if it causes more problems for him on the set?"

Trent shook his head. "Look, it was *his* message. I really think we should tell him about it," he said.

Nancy stared at Trent, trying to remember something.

"Okay, we won't mention it," Trent said, obviously misinterpreting her intense expression. "But only because you say so. Let's get out of here. I feel as though this creep climbed right in the window."

I know just what you mean, Trent, she thought. The blackmailer's getting too close for comfort. Nancy looked at Trent and slowly leaned forward to kiss his cheek.

"Thanks," he said, smiling and stroking her hair.

"I really feel I'm getting to know you, Trent," Nancy said. She stood up. "We'd better go join the others."

The Jacksons and George were having breakfast on the sunporch.

"Hey, everyone," Nancy said as she walked into the sunny, plant-filled room. She dropped into a seat and poured herself a glass of juice.

Trent put his jacket on the back of the chair next to Nancy's, then sat down beside her. He greeted everyone with a cheerful good morning.

"Feeling better today?" James asked Nancy.

Nancy nodded. "I slept like the dead," she said, and immediately regretted her choice of words. Bad joke, she thought.

"That was quite an ordeal you went through, Nancy. This has got to stop. As if harming my family and me wasn't enough, now this black-mailer has even begun harming innocent by-standers," James said. "Maybe we should call in the police now. It's gone too far. My reputation is nothing compared with the lives and safety of those dear to me."

Raye Jackson looked at her husband and smiled wearily. "I don't know what the right thing to do is, James," she said quietly. "But I do know you'll be ruined if this gets out. We must keep trying."

"We will," Nancy insisted. "I only have a few minutes for breakfast this morning, actually, because George and I have a lot of work to do," Nancy said, helping herself to a corn muffin.

"We do? Like what?" George demanded.

"Well, the blackmailer doesn't realize it, but for the first time, we have a decent clue to work with."

James sat up straight. "What is it, Nancy?"

"The blackmailer had to be on the set after everyone was dismissed early yesterday—during the time I was poking around in Lori's trailer. This person also had to be free—and strong enough—to tie me up, load me into Lori's Maserati, and drive me out of town. It won't be hard to find out who has an alibi and who doesn't."

"Using the process of elimination," Lori guessed.

"That's right," Nancy agreed.

Trent interrupted. "But that would work only if we knew what time Nancy was kidnapped."

Nancy grinned. "I do—or pretty close to it."

She remembered that in Lori's trailer, a few minutes before she'd blacked out, she'd watched the neon numbers on the Elvis Presley clock change from 4:03 to 4:04.

She had established a starting time for the alibis she was looking for. Then she thought back to the Maserati. As she was waking in the trunk, she'd heard the radio announcer say it was four fifty-seven. So she had a lock on the time when she had been alone with the kidnapper.

The group seemed amazed as Nancy explained her thinking.

"Incredible!" Lori exclaimed. "She's drugged, tied up in the trunk of a car, but she knows exactly how long she was out of it."

"That's Nancy," George said proudly.

"So, let's start with David," Nancy said. "Anyone see him between four and five o'clock?"

The group looked at one another. No one said a word. Then Lori mumbled sheepishly, "Uh, I did."

She sneaked a guilty peek at her mother, then at her father. "We spent the afternoon together."

"Lori, you *promised* us you wouldn't see David anymore," Mrs. Jackson said.

Lori swallowed hard. "I know. But I couldn't help it. My feelings for him don't just go away like that." She snapped her fingers.

"Okay, well, that clears David," Nancy announced.

Lori smiled. Her parents looked grim.

"Next up—Danielle. Anyone see her?"

This time, James answered. "Danielle left the set with me. We spent the rest of the afternoon going over some effects."

Nancy nodded. "Okay. That's good. She's off the hook."

"Wow, Nancy." Lori laughed. "I'm glad I'm not on your suspect list."

"What makes you think you aren't?" Nancy joked.

"So who's left as a suspect?" Trent asked, ignoring Nancy's joke.

Nancy took a deep breath. "Susie," she said. "I saw her leave the set—or act like she was leaving—before I went into Lori's trailer. Did anyone see her after four o'clock?"

James shook his head. "I called her while I was working with Danielle. I think it was around four-thirty, but all I got was her answering machine."

"Strange," Nancy said. "She told me she was going back to her office to catch up on phone calls."

"You know," Trent said, "I saw Susie yesterday afternoon. But it wasn't between four and five. It was about five-thirty. I was dropping a few things off at Galaxie Towers, where her offices are. She was rushing into the building."

"That's it, then," Nancy said. "Susie was out of the office at four-thirty and came rushing back at five-thirty. I'll call her and see if she comes up with an alibi."

"Nancy, you don't really think Susie is capable of blackmailing me, planning all those accidents, and sending those high-tech treats, do you?" James asked. "And she definitely doesn't need the money."

"That's true," Nancy said. "But we know she *does* have the money to hire a cast of thousands to carry out every accident or send any threat you've received. Plus, she hasn't been hiding her enthusiasm over the mishaps on the set. Each one just spells more profits in her mind. Don't forget how quick she was to publicize Lori's shooting."

"I couldn't forget," James said. "Still, as much as I dislike Susie, I just can't believe she's the one." He paused for a moment. "Unless she's out for revenge." Nancy nodded as she and James shared a look. She was sorry to mislead him this way, but there was no way, at that moment, that she could tell him who the real blackmailer was.

There was silence as the news sank in around the table. It was broken by the doorbell ringing. The intercom buzzed, and Liam announced that Susie Yaeger had just arrived.

"She's got a lot of nerve setting foot in this house," Raye proclaimed indignantly.

"Don't say a word," Nancy warned.

Liam brought Susie out to the sunporch. Nancy could see the woman was trying to seem calm but that underneath she was very upset. She pulled off her stylish black beret and tossed it on an empty chair.

"Susie. Perhaps you could have called before coming over," James said, clearly trying to keep his own emotions in check.

"What I have to tell you needs to be said in person," Susie said.

James flashed a look at Nancy. "Should we talk in private?"

Susie shook her head. "No. This affects Lori and Trent, too, so I might as well tell you all. *Dangerous Loves* is finished."

A dark look crossed James's face. "What do you mean? We still have key scenes to film."

Susie sighed, looking sorry for James for the first time. She reached out and put a hand on his sleeve. "I'm sorry, James, but those scenes will never be shot. *Dangerous Loves* is through. We're canceling the production. The insurance company called me. They're jacking up the premiums because of all the accidents, and we can't afford the escalated rates."

Nancy looked from one shocked face to another. "Can't we raise the money somehow?" James asked.

Susie shook her head. "I made some calls. The backers say they've already put too much money into this production. James, I'm sorry," Susie said. "There's no way we can finish the movie without insurance. And there's no way we can afford the insurance we now require."

"I can't wait to see *this* in the papers tomorrow morning," James said.

"You won't—unless *you* call them," Susie said

softly. "I haven't told a soul. And I won't. I give you my word." She turned to leave. "I've had a headache since yesterday," she murmured. "Even a two-hour massage didn't get rid of it." She left, absentmindedly neglecting to say goodbye.

"I can't believe it," Lori said. "We worked so hard—for nothing."

"It's okay, honey," Raye said. "There will be other movies."

"Do you still think Susie will go through with her blackmail threats?" George asked Nancy. "I mean, now that the production is off, she couldn't expect James to come up with ten million dollars. This insurance rate hike is no good for her, either."

Nancy looked at George and nodded pensively.

"This is really depressing," Trent said. He got up and grabbed his jacket from the back of his chair. "I think I'll go home now. See you later, everyone. James, let's talk about this later," he said as he left.

James put his head down on the table, and his wife walked over to him and rubbed his back. Lori began to cry quietly, and George and Nancy glanced at each other awkwardly.

The doorbell rang for a second time a few minutes later. Liam buzzed James on the intercom. "Ms. Yaeger's back," he announced.

In the next instant, she came into the room.

"I'm not staying," Susie said. "I just came for my hat. I left it here."

She looked around the room, spotted the beret lying on the chair where she'd thrown it, and scooped it up.

Susie turned back, with one foot out the door. "I'm sorry about the movie, James," she said sincerely. "I wish it could be different."

"Me, too, Susie," James said sadly.

The intercom buzzed. "Yes?" Raye answered.

"Call for Mr. Jackson," Liam's voice said on the other end of the intercom.

"I don't want to be disturbed."

"I think you should take this one," Liam insisted.

James sighed, then walked over to the phone, hit the speaker button, and sank into a white wicker chair. "James Jackson here," he said.

A strange, metallic noise came over the speaker. "It's me," the person said.

Everyone knew it was the blackmailer. Nancy noted the caller was using a voice distortion device. "The movie's dead," the person said. "If you don't want to die too, pay up."

The caller directed James to drop off the money at the 1945 station wagon in the vintage-car parking lot on the set of *Dangerous Loves* exactly at midnight. "And bring Nancy Drew with you," the voice said.

"Nancy?" Lori repeated.

"I don't think I can do that," James said. "This is between you and me."

Nancy grabbed James's arm and shook her head. "It's okay," she mouthed. "I want to come."

"You'd better bring her," the distorted voice insisted. "Along with the money. All hundreds. No cops. No excuses. Or this time someone really will get hurt."

Chapter

Thirteen

SUSIE WAS THE FIRST to speak. "James, what is going on here? Why didn't you tell me?"

"I couldn't tell anyone," he answered simply.

Raye Jackson embraced her husband. "You two can't meet that blackmailer alone," she said, near tears. "Something could happen to you both."

Nancy waved her hand. "Don't worry, Raye. If this is done right, it will work."

"And if it isn't?" George asked,

Nancy threw her a look. She didn't want anyone thinking too hard about that possibility.

George continued to question her friend. "I thought you agreed the blackmailer probably wouldn't go through with the threats now that the film has been canceled."

"That was when I still wanted to think the blackmailer might be Susie," Nancy said quietly.

"Me!" Susie gasped.

Nancy nodded. "I was going to ask if you had an alibi for the time I was kidnapped yesterday."

Susie looked as if she might faint. "I was getting a massage all afternoon. It was a two o'clock appointment, and it lasted two hours. If you call my masseuse, she'll confirm it for you."

"I'm sure she will," Nancy said. She looked slowly around the table. "I know who the blackmailer is," she said. If she hadn't been certain earlier that morning, she was positive now.

All eyes turned to Nancy. "It's Trent Marino," she announced. She explained how she'd watched Trent surf the Web like an expert. By his own admission, or boast, he knew cars inside and out from his research for *Me and My Rolls*. And she knew from watching *A Taste to Die For* that he knew plenty about poison.

"A real Renaissance man," she said with a shiver.

"But what finally tipped me off was when he argued with me about an E-mail message directed to me—it was in your mailbox this morning, James." He started to speak, but Nancy quieted him with a wave of her hand. "It doesn't matter what the message was, James. But Trent said he thought you should know about, as he put it, 'this latest E-mail threat.' But even though Trent knew I was investigating the blackmail, none of us ever mentioned the E-mail aspect of the case to him."

"I just can't believe it," James repeated to Nancy an hour later. He kept his eyes on the road, steering the car with one hand. "Trent Marino is my partner—my friend."

Nancy nodded. "Believe me, I didn't suspect him at first." Nancy wasn't about to tell James that she had almost fallen for Trent. She didn't want to believe it herself.

The sedan followed the now-familiar stretch of highway between the Jacksons' mansion and the set. "I know that you're right," James said. "But I wish you weren't. This means my whole relationship with him has been nothing but a lie."

While James drove, Nancy went over the details of the rendezvous she'd planned with the blackmailer for later that evening. Everyone had agreed it was time to call the police. They immediately developed a plan. Officers in plainclothes would be dropped off at the studio, and they would be waiting in hiding not far from the old station wagon.

James pulled into the set parking lot and steered the car into the director's spot. "Well, here we are," he said to Nancy. "Are you ready?"

Nancy took a deep breath, then said, "Yes."

"Nancy, are you sure you're going to be all right? Can you really talk to Trent without tipping him off?"

"James, please don't worry," she said. "I've

been in this type of situation before. Will *you* be able to carry it off?"

The director waved his hand in the air. "Oh, me. I'll just be my normal nasty self."

Nancy eyed him. "Nasty?"

James nodded. "I guess I haven't really been very nice to Trent over the years. It's a director thing. We stomp all over the writers' scripts without once asking their opinion." He smiled wryly and shook his head as if to chastise himself.

"Maybe so," Nancy said. "But that doesn't excuse what he's done to you."

"I know that," the director said. "I'm just trying to understand how this happened. I'll see you later tonight, Nancy. Be careful."

"I will, James. You, too."

He hurried off to the set, leaving Nancy alone by the car. She was about to go look for Trent, when she saw his car pull into the lot. She forced a smile and waved.

Trent tooted his horn and waved back as he parked. As he got out of his car, he gave her one of his wide smiles.

What's he grinning about? Nancy thought with dread. Well, I guess I'd be smiling, too, if I thought I was getting away with the scam of a lifetime—and a cool ten million dollars.

"Hey," Trent said as he approached Nancy. She was afraid for a moment that he was about to pull her into a hug.

But he didn't. "How's James?" he asked.

"Things got worse and worse after you left," Nancy said. The hot sun beat down on them in the parking lot. "James got another phone call. It seems the blackmailer still wants the money after all. James is supposed to leave it in the vintage car lot tonight."

"You're kidding."

Nancy shook he head.

"So, where's James going to get the money?"

Though she'd never mentioned it to him, Trent had to know James didn't have the money. Nancy had to tell him something good, something to make him believe that James really had the cash. Otherwise, he might guess he was being set up and not show up that night at all.

Nancy had already prepared an explanation. "James just heard from the bank this morning. We got them to agree to lend him the ten million against his house and future residuals on film projects."

"James is getting a *loan?*" Trent exclaimed.

Nancy nodded. "He knows he might lose the house—but he'll get the blackmailer off his back."

"But what about Susie?" Trent asked.

"Turns out she had an alibi, after all," Nancy said. "I'm willing to keep on investigating, but I think James is near the breaking point. He'd rather pay the money than have anyone else be injured—or worse."

Trent shook his head. "I really feel sorry for the guy. I wish there was something I could do."

It was all Nancy could do to conceal her true feelings as she said, "Oh, you've done enough already."

That evening Nancy stood beside James Jackson in a circle of light. They stared out over the dark shapes of the 1940s cars, waiting to get a glimpse of the blackmailer. Mr. Jackson nervously flexed and unflexed his grip around the handle of a lawyer's huge attaché case, which was meant to contain ten million dollars in cash.

Actually, there was no money in the case. James had visited no banks that morning, as Nancy had told Trent. He hadn't taken out a loan. The bills in the case were props used in *Money to Burn*, a film about a counterfeiting ring that Susie had produced the year before.

The bills looked reasonably real at first glance, but on close inspection, it was easy to see the cash was phony. But Trent would be opening the case in the darkness, and if he didn't have a chance to look carefully at the money, Nancy was sure her plan would work.

Even if he discovered they were counterfeit, it would be too late. Police were positioned in a tight circle around the perimeter of the parking lot. Also, somewhere among the police, George was watching. And Nancy was glad her friend had insisted on coming.

The temperature had dropped as night set in, and Nancy shivered slightly in her jeans and long-sleeved cotton turtleneck. She wished she'd worn a jacket.

James looked at his watch. Its face glowed in the darkness. "It's two minutes after twelve. Is he coming or isn't he?"

"Shhh," Nancy said. She'd heard a sound from behind the station wagon.

"Hello, James."

The voice that rang out over the set was the same distorted one that they had heard on the phone earlier that morning. Trent was using his gadget again, covering his tracks as he went for the money.

"Hello," James answered nervously.

"I see you've brought Nancy with you," Trent called from where he hid. "You didn't bring along any police friends, did you?"

"Of course not," James said.

"I'm glad Nancy's here," Trent went on. "Because in case you *did* bring police, she's my insurance policy. Come on over here, Nancy, very, very slowly."

So that was why he'd insisted she come. Nancy should have figured he'd have some kind of plan to protect himself from a double cross.

Nancy started to step forward.

"No!" James's voice rang out. He grabbed Nancy and pulled her back. "I can't let you go." He lowered his voice. "I was responsible for one death many years ago. I won't be responsible for another."

Nancy sucked in her breath. "I have to go. This is the only way to bring him in. Please. I can handle myself."

She shook free of his grip and stepped forward. "I'm ready," she called into the darkness.

"Good. I knew I could count on you. Now, Nancy, bring me the attaché case," the voice directed her.

"Just follow my voice. I'm behind the station wagon."

Nancy took a deep breath, picked up the attaché case and slowly moved away from the pool of light and from James.

"That's it," the voice encouraged. "Keep coming."

Nancy turned back and looked one last time at James. She continued to follow Trent's voice. In the dark, she could hardly see where she was going. Trent, however, seemed to know the terrain despite the blackness. He directed Nancy expertly around crates and film equipment as if with radar. Unable to see, she felt at his mercy.

At last, however, Nancy realized where he was taking her—to the soda shop set, which Trent had called his special place.

Once they were inside, he stepped out of the darkness and into a dim ribbon of light. His face now had none of the charm that had caught Nancy's attention the day she met him.

"Hello, Nancy." This time, Trent spoke in his natural voice. He gave Nancy a smile. There was something in his right hand. Nancy squinted.

She could see the glint of metal. He was holding a small handgun.

"Trent," Nancy said.

"You don't seem surprised to see me."

"I'm not."

Trent shrugged. "You *are* a clever detective. But it doesn't matter, as long as I get what I came here for." He held out his free hand. "Give me the money, please."

Nancy gripped the handle. She couldn't let him look in the case—not until she'd gotten rid of the handgun. The minute he discovered the money was fake, he'd be furious. There was no telling what he'd do to her then.

"Just a minute," Nancy said, stalling for time. "Can I ask you something?"

"If you make it quick," he answered. "Go ahead."

"Well, first of all, why? You can't need the money that badly."

Trent laughed. "Oh, Nancy, *everyone* needs money. Some people, like James, for instance, need money to support their lavish life-styles. I have different priorities. I need money to make my own films. You see, I'm tired, very tired, of watching James ruin everything I've ever written."

"Trent, what are you talking about? The critics have raved about all the movies you've made with James."

Trent scowled. "The critics! Sure, it's nice that they like the films, but box-office bombs don't pay the rent. I'm sure these films would have succeeded if James had shown an ounce of respect for my work. But you saw him. He changes my ideas on nothing more than a whim. I mean it, Nancy. I think he does it sometimes just because he can, just to show me that it's his film and not mine."

He sounded bitter. Nancy knew there was at least a little truth in what Trent was saying. James had admitted as much himself.

But Trent's angry emotions were showing. They were bound to cloud his cool control, giving Nancy just the window of opportunity she needed.

"Why didn't you just stop working with him?" Nancy asked. She hoped to draw him further into his story.

"Don't be naive, Nancy. In Hollywood, you work with whom you know, whom you have connections with. If I could, I'd be working with half a dozen talented directors. But they think of me as James's writer. They have no idea that I can do better than write one bomb after another."

Nancy changed the subject. "There's something I've wanted to know," she said. "How did you find out about the Rapid Island incident?"

Trent waved his right hand in the air. The handgun shone in the thin beam of light.

"Oh, that was easy. He never told me about what happened at Rapid Island, but he would mention the place every so often. And just as I found out about you when you told me you were from the Chicago area, all I had to do was hack my way into the Rapid Island police records. Although the records didn't say he was driving the night of the accident, I figured he must have been. I had overheard Susie talking to James about her friend who had died that night, and I sensed her hostility. I took a chance that he had actually been the driver, and it turned out I was right."

"And how did you pull off the prop gun mishap with Lori and the car accident with the stuntwoman and me?"

Trent laughed. "Believe it or not, I didn't. As far as I know, those really *were* accidents. Fate did all my hard work for me. All I had to do was leave computer messages claiming responsibility." He let out a nasty laugh. "I had James so freaked out, he would have believed anything."

"And the snake for Raye? And the poison lipstick?" Nancy asked.

Trent sighed. "Well, those I *did* set up."

"Trent, one last question and we can be finished here. What makes you think you'll be able to just take this money and go make a movie with it? I mean everyone will know it was you before too long."

Trent's face twisted. "I'm not worried about that. You're the only eyewitness—and you won't be around to prove it. Now, give me the case."

Nancy shivered. Trent was planning on murdering her; she had to do something. She stepped forward, holding out the case. As Trent reached for it, Nancy flung the case at Trent, aiming for his weapon hand.

Trent batted the case away easily, but his gun fell, just out of the light. "You shouldn't have done that," he said.

Then he came at her. She stood her ground, blocking his arm as he reached for her. She threw a false punch to distract him, hoping to catch him with a kick.

But he was fast. He grabbed her foot and yanked, sending her sprawling. In the next instant, he was on top of her. He was stronger than she was, and he jammed his hand over her mouth. Before she knew it, he had a wet, smelly piece of cloth over her mouth and nose.

Nancy recognized the smell; it was chloroform. If she breathed in, it would knock her out.

She struggled, twisting her head, trying desperately to get away from the rag so she could steal another breath.

But Trent's hand stayed firmly over her face. Finally, she couldn't hold her breath any longer.

She gasped and took in a big lungful of chloroform. One more breath, and she was going to fall into a deep sleep.

Chapter

Fourteen

NANCY LASHED OUT, aiming her fingers for Trent's eyes.

He shrieked as two of Nancy's fingers connected with his eyeballs. He tumbled backward and hit the old-fashioned soda counter, which collapsed behind him. Glass bottles rained down on him.

He yelled as they hit him in the face.

Nancy seized the moment. She quickly stood and shook her head to clear it. She felt woozy from the chloroform, but she knew she had to hit him while he was down and keep him down until help arrived.

Trent held up his hand, which was bleeding from being cut by a shattered bottle. "I'm sorry it's come to this, Nancy. We were friends just a day ago . . ."

Nancy laughed. "Friends? After you left me tied up in the trunk of Lori's car by the side of the road?"

She aimed a karate chop at the hand that still held the chloroform rag. But Trent twisted away and jumped to his feet. He was coming toward Nancy with the rag again.

Where are the police? Nancy thought, feeling a wave of desperation. Why are they taking so long?

Just then she heard a familiar "Keeee-yah!" George flew through the air and shot a sidekick at Trent that knocked him on his back.

George jumped on him, trying to pin back his arms, when Nancy called, "George, look out!"

But it was too late. George had managed to grab one arm, but with his free hand Trent slapped the chloroform rag over George's nose and mouth. Caught off guard, she loosened her grasp on his other arm.

Nancy leaped on Trent, hitting him as hard as she could. But she could see George inhale once, twice—and she was gone.

Trent pushed Nancy off, and finding his gun near where he sat, he pointed it at Nancy, then grabbed George by the arm and pulled her limp body toward him.

"George?" Nancy cried. When her friend didn't respond, Nancy took a step toward her.

"Don't come any closer," Trent warned her, his gun aimed at George. "Take one step and I'll kill her. And don't think I won't, Nancy. I've come too far to let you mess things up for me now."

In the distance, lights glared. "Trent Marino, give yourself up. This is the police," came a voice over a bullhorn.

"Tell them I have George," Trent ordered Nancy.

"Leave him alone!" Nancy called out into the darkness. "He's got George, and she's unconscious."

"And I won't hesitate to kill her," he shouted.

Nancy stared at him for a second. "Please, don't do anything," she called to the police. "He's armed, and he'll kill her."

"Okay, Nancy," Trent quietly said. "Now you just push that money over in this direction." He indicated the attaché case. "Then George and I will be on our way."

She edged the case toward him. He motioned for her to back off. Then he grasped its handle, hoisted George over his shoulder, and slipped into the darkness.

Nancy and the police coordinated their search. The cops would circle wide behind the area where Trent had disappeared, hoping to catch him before he made his escape. Nancy needed to get to Trent and George before he realized the money wasn't real.

The set was dark and quiet. Trent was being as

careful and silent as Nancy. Then she heard a muffled gasping, like someone trying to catch a breath without being heard. Maybe Trent was having a hard time carrying George and the attaché case together.

This was it, Nancy thought. She'd have to be extra careful.

She heard the gasping sound again, and it seemed to come from behind a plywood wall at Nancy's left. She shoved hard against the wall and heard a cracking sound as it crashed on top of Trent and George.

Trent scrambled frantically to get out from under the pile of broken plywood.

Nancy didn't give him time to recover. He had dropped the gun. In his stuggle to regain his hold on George, the attaché case, and the gun, Trent left himself vulnerable to Nancy's quick maneuvering. As he reached down, she leaped on his back, knocking him flat.

"You almost had me fooled, Trent," Nancy said, twisting his arm behind his back. "Maybe after you get out of jail, you might try a career as an actor."

The police descended within moments. Nancy handed Trent over to the officers and fell to George's side. She saw that there was a bruise forming on George's forehead where the plywood had hit her, but she was blissfully unaware of it, since she was still unconscious from the chloroform. George was going to be pretty unhappy over sleeping through the exciting part, Nancy thought with a smile.

"You have the right to remain silent. . . ." Nancy heard an officer reading Trent his rights.

James Jackson walked over slowly and stood in front of Trent. "So it really was you," he said quietly. "I didn't want to believe it."

Trent stared at James blankly.

Three officers escorted Trent in the direction of the parking lot where half a dozen squad cars were now parked, red lights flashing and radios crackling.

The paramedics tended to George. One of them told Nancy that George would need to be examined by a doctor at the hospital. She was groggy but awake, and she squeezed Nancy's hand.

"Thanks, pal, I owe you," George said with a weak smile.

"No way, George. *I* owe *you!*" Nancy said emphatically.

"All right, all right. We're even, then." George waved as the attendants wheeled her off to the ambulance.

After everyone had gone, James and Nancy stood alone on the ruined set. James stared around him. "Look at this mess. I guess the destruction of the set doesn't matter." He sighed. *"Dangerous Loves* is already dead in the water."

Nancy felt for him. Even with Trent in police custody, it wasn't a very happy ending for James.

His blackmailer had turned out to be one of his most trusted colleagues, the movie was canceled, and his future was looking pretty grim, too.

"Come on, James," Nancy said. "It's been a long night, and there's nothing we can do now. Let's go home."

Chapter

Fifteen

"Here's to *Dangerous Loves*!" James declared happily. He popped the top on another can of soda and poured some into a glass, which he handed to Susie. "Have a drink," he said.

"Don't mind if I do," she answered, toasting James.

Nancy took it all in from the dance floor, where she was rocking with a gorgeous actor friend of Lori's named Rex. Music poured from four huge speakers. George was hanging out with the deejay, cuing up CDs. She smiled and threw Nancy a thumbs-up sign. The only reminder of George's ordeal was the greenish bruise on her forehead.

The party for *Dangerous Loves* was certainly a hit. And why not? The movie was back in production again.

The day after Trent's arrest, the story had hit the papers. No one knew who leaked the story, and Susie swore it wasn't she. Whoever it had been, as news of what really happened on the set circulated, Susie had been able to go back to the insurance company and get the insurance reinstated. So, the movie was a go again.

Nancy looked around, feeling happy that things had worked out in the end. Lori and David were in a corner, arguing yet again. Danielle was slipping ice cubes with plastic ants frozen into them into people's glasses. Raye Jackson acted the hostess, greeting guests, ordering caterers around, straightening the bartender's bow tie.

James Jackson stood on a chair and gently hit his glass with a fork. Of course, it was impossible to hear the sound over the music, but Nancy motioned to George, who cut the volume.

The director raised his glass in a toast. "None of us would be here today if it hadn't been for Nancy Drew. So let's all give her a big hand."

The crowd cheered her, clapping and whistling and shouting "Bravo!"

"She's the one who's made it possible for me to finish *Dangerous Loves*," he continued. "And of course, there's Susie, who put us back in business. My wife, Raye, who has been such a support through all this—and all of you." He held up his glass and toasted the crowd.

Trent may finally make a lot of money on his

screenplay, Nancy thought grimly. But he'll have to enjoy it from behind prison bars.

Nancy raised a glass to make her own toast: "I want to thank George, who helped me out on this and never complained about the bruises."

Everyone laughed. George rolled her eyes and turned up the volume. Then she walked over to join Nancy. "Now that the danger's over, Nan, how about we try surfing?"

Nancy and George would be leaving the next day for a flight back to River Heights. But Nancy knew she'd be back. James had insisted that she return to Hollywood for a minor part in his next film. And this time, he promised, there would be no crazy stunts and no crowd scenes.

Nancy's next case:

When Ned's invited to study at the Rocky Isle Marine Institute in Maine, Nancy joins him as a volunteer at the facility's aquarium. But Ned fears that a handsome tour guide is creating serious waves in their relationship. Nancy, however, has to deal with a different kind of storm— one threatening to destroy the entire institute. Already in dire financial straits, the aquarium has lost its prized baby dolphin, and someone's demanding a million-dollar ransom. Is it Matt Folton, animal-rights activist and major TV star? Nancy suspects that a deadlier human shark is on the prowl, and she'll take any risk— even act as bait—to ensure the dolphin's safe return . . . in *Natural Enemies,* Case #121 in The Nancy Drew Files™.

R·L·STINE'S
GHOSTS OF FEAR STREET®

A MINSTREL® BOOK

Simon & Schuster Mail Order
200 Old Tappan Rd., Old Tappan, N.J. 07675
Please send me the books I have checked above. I am enclosing $_____ (please add
$0.75 to cover the postage and handling for each order. Please add appropriate sales
tax). Send check or money order—no cash or C.O.D.'s please. Allow up to six weeks
for delivery. For purchase over $10.00 you may use VISA: card number, expiration
date and customer signature must be included.

POCKET
B O O K S

Name _____

Address _____

City _____ State/Zip _____

VISA Card # _____ Exp.Date _____

Signature _____ 1180-15